CO-AYR-525

"It's all right. We're alone now,"

Bruce said as he reached for Helena. "Darling..."
Bruce protested as she evaded him.

"You should call me Miss Walker," Helena said
coolly.

"I do—when others are around. But when we're
alone I'll call you my lovely Helena."

He said the words in a voice that sent shivers through
her. But she clung to her resolve. "Since we're not
going to be alone again, there'll be no occasion for
hyperbole."

Bruce winced. "Must you talk as though I were a
student?"

"Mr. Venables, did you want to discuss school
matters?"

"Helena! Why are you acting this way?"

"I'm acting as I should have from the start. Our
behavior was unprofessional."

Bruce ran his hand through his hair. "I'll grant that
trying to kiss you wasn't in accordance with staff
etiquette, but I couldn't help myself. I can't stop
thinking about kissing you." He smiled persuasively.
"So what are we going to do about it?"

Dear Reader,

The holiday season is upon us and what better present to give or receive than a Silhouette Romance novel. And what a wonderful lineup we have in store for you!

Each month in 1992, we're proud to present our WRITTEN IN THE STARS series, which focuses on the hero and his astrological sign. Our December title draws the series to its heavenly conclusion when sexy Sagittarius Bruce Venables meets the woman destined to be his love in Lucy Gordon's *Heaven and Earth*.

This month also continues Stella Bagwell's HEARTLAND HOLIDAYS trilogy. Christmas bells turn to wedding bells for another Gallagher sibling. Join Nicholas and Allison as they find good reason to seek out the mistletoe.

To round out the month we have enchanting, heartwarming love stories from Carla Cassidy, Linda Varner and Moyra Tarling. And, as an extra special treat, we have a tale of passion from Helen R. Myers, with a dark, mysterious hero who will definitely take your breath away.

In the months to come, watch for Silhouette Romance stories by many more of your favorite authors, including Diana Palmer, Annette Broadrick, Elizabeth August and Marie Ferrarella.

The authors and editors at Silhouette Romance love to hear from our readers, and we'd love to hear from *you!*

Happy reading from all of us at Silhouette!

Anne Canadeo
Senior Editor

HEAVEN AND EARTH
Lucy Gordon

Silhouette
ROMANCE™
Published by Silhouette Books New York
America's Publisher of Contemporary Romance

SILHOUETTE BOOKS
300 E. 42nd St., New York, N.Y. 10017

HEAVEN AND EARTH

Copyright © 1992 by Lucy Gordon

LOVE AND THE SAGITTARIUS MAN
Copyright © 1992 by Harlequin Enterprises B.V.

ISBN: 0-373-08904-X

First Silhouette Books printing December 1992

All the characters in this book have no existence outside the imagination of the author and have no relation whatsoever to anyone bearing the same name or names. They are not even distantly inspired by any individual known or unknown to the author, and all incidents are pure invention.

®: Trademark used under license and registered in the United States Patent and Trademark Office and in other countries.

Printed in the U.S.A.

LUCY GORDON

Virgo is the writer's sign, so it always seemed likely that I'd become one. What wasn't so destined was that I should marry a Sagittarius—of all the signs in the zodiac, Virgo and Sagittarius are the worst combination! But I decided to take the risk, and I've never regretted it.

I was excited to write about the Sagittarius man—not only because he's the kind I know best, but because he's so varied. He'll read intellectual volumes one minute and watch cartoons the next! He enjoys life, and if you're lucky enough to find one who's finished his roving, he's the best kind of husband.

We've been married twenty-two happy years, so maybe, as my fictional Sagittarius hero observes, the stars don't know everything!

SAGITTARIUS

Ninth sign of the Zodiac
November 23 to December 20
Symbol: Archer
Planet: Jupiter
Element: Fire
Stone: Turquoise
Color: Purple
Metal: Tin
Flower: Narcissus
Lucky Day: Thursday
Countries: Spain, Australia, Hungary
Cities: Avignon, Toledo, Naples

Famous Sagittarians

Kirk Douglas
Steven Spielberg
Walt Disney
Mark Twain

Tina Turner
Bette Midler
Jane Fonda
Louisa May Alcott

★

Chapter One

"That has to be the most unbelievable decision I've ever heard," Helena stormed. "It's disgraceful—an outrage. There must be something we can do."

"I doubt it," Jane observed wryly. "It was all settled behind closed doors before we were informed."

They were alone in the staff common room of Edenbrook School, but not for long. Any moment the rest of the staff would stream in, full of surprise, pleasure or indignation at the name of the new acting headmaster.

"'Acting' my foot," Helena fumed. "Since when is Bruce Venables anybody's understudy?"

"Does that mean you know him?" Jane inquired curiously.

"I—no—I've never actually met him. But I've heard of his reputation. Who hasn't?"

"There are some who'll say he's an acquisition," Jane pointed out. "He stands very high in academic circles."

"Too high. That's my whole point. This 'acting' business is just whitewash. He'll be confirmed as soon as they can make it look decent. It's positively wicked for him to take the job only two days after George became ill. George gave years to this school. He made it one of the best in the country and he wanted to serve out his full term. Now he's kicked out the minute he shows the slightest sign of weakness."

"But it wasn't a slight sign. It was a massive heart attack," Jane reminded her. "It'll be months before he can come back."

"It'll be never," Helena said angrily. "They're not going to throw Bruce Venables out to let George return."

She threw herself into a chair, brooding. A lock of honey-colored, wavy hair tumbled out of its pins about her face and she pushed it back, securing it firmly. She had a rich, glorious mane, which was always kept severely in check during school hours.

George was there in her mind, chuckling as he'd done the day he'd appointed her junior history mistress three years ago. "You'll have to keep those ravishing locks of yours under wraps," he'd said. "Can't have the senior boys daydreaming through class."

Dear old George! she thought. No one could take offense at his frankness because his air of an absentminded Father Christmas cast a benign cloak over everything. He'd been dear to her from the day she'd arrived at Edenbrook, with impeccable credentials, but short on experience. She hadn't really expected to get the job, but George wasn't like any other head-

master. Edenbrook was his own loving creation and
he'd applied his own highly individual standards to
choosing staff. He'd glanced briefly at her impressive
scholastic results, then demanded her ideas about a
series of great historical characters. His own opinions
had been pithy and unorthodox.

"Can't stand him," he'd declared loftily about
some revered icon from the seventeenth century.
"They say he was a great general—thoroughly silly
man, in my view."

Emboldened, Helena had dared voice some of her
own franker views. George had cheered her on and
they'd laughed together. He'd passed over more experienced candidates to appoint her, insisting that she
would be a "breath of fresh air." She'd been awed by
such a big jump in her career, but George had guided
her early footsteps, and always been there to offer
kindly advice. Gradually she'd come to see him as the
father she'd never had.

Then he'd collapsed. And in two days his place was
taken by a brilliant young academic who would
doubtless set about remodeling Edenbrook in order to
impose his own personality. For a moment Helena's
fierce sense of loyalty to George made her consider
resigning in protest, but she dismissed the idea. She
must be here to fight for George's right to return.

Secretly she was conscious that her anger had another cause, one she wasn't so ready to admit. It was
true, as she'd told Jane, that she'd never met Bruce
Venables, but still, she wasn't totally impartial. A few
months earlier she'd become an author. Her first book
about Charles Darwin, aimed at children, had appeared under the pseudonym of Caroline Ross. She'd
lacked the confidence to tell anyone about it, even

George, hoping that the book might be enough of a success to enable her to claim authorship with pride.

But Bruce Venables had savaged it in an educational publication. "It's a pity this book was ever published," he'd written. "The author has tried to make a complicated subject accessible to children. This is a laudable ambition but unfortunately she's gone too far, and simplified everything to the point of uselessness. I should be sorry to see this work in any school library."

The words had gone through Helena like a knife. She'd withdrawn into herself, telling no one of her authorship. Her publisher had called to say that a wholesaler that supplied school libraries, had canceled an order.

And that was that. The book had died of shame. Even now Helena's cheeks burned as she thought of that criticism. She pictured Bruce Venables, secure in his literary and academic achievements, master of this, professor of that, murdering her infant aspirations with casual cruelty.

And now he was to be here, in this school, working even more cruelly to oust George. And she herself was in danger of discovery by this man who thought so contemptuously of her abilities. The thought sent shivers through her.

That afternoon she left the school as soon as the final bell sounded, and hurried home. Her flat consisted of three rooms on the upper floor of a house whose owner occupied the floor downstairs. Mrs. Carter was a widow who currently spent many of her evenings visiting her elderly father in hospital, and Helena had gladly agreed to keep an eye on Sally, her twelve-year-old daughter. She had no experience with children outside a school, but the task was made easier by the fact that Sally, a pupil at Edenbrook, admired her extravagantly, and had adopted her as a role model.

Tonight there was no sign of Sally when she entered, and she was glad of it. She needed time to pull herself together. She'd thought her disappointment over the book was dead and buried, but the knowledge that Bruce Venables would soon be a real presence in her life had brought all the pain alive again, and with it came the revival of another pain.

Helena had never known her parents. She'd been born illegitimate and her mother had died soon after, without ever revealing her lover's name. Helena had been brought up by her mother's much older sister and her husband, chilly, old-fashioned people who'd disapproved of her very existence. They'd done what they saw as their duty, but there had been little affection in the home. Helena had grown up obscurely blaming herself for their indifference, and trying to win their love by doing better. At school she'd always been at the top of the class, passing her exams with flying colors. They'd praised her conscientiously, but there'd never been the outpouring of spontaneous joy she'd longed for.

She was twenty-four now, and saw little of her uncle and aunt, who lived in another part of the country. But even now she cherished the hope that the next achievement might break through their reserve. Perhaps the book might have done it. But that hope, too, had been dashed.

Presently Mrs. Carter put her head around the door. "I'm just off to the hospital," she said. "Is it all right for Sally to come in tonight? I've told her not to be a nuisance.''

''I'm never a nuisance,'' Sally declared indignantly, coming in and seating herself at the table. ''Am I, Miss Walker?''

''Nothing that I can't cope with,'' Helena declared with a smile. ''Don't rush back, Mrs. Carter. Sally will be fine with me.''

As soon as they were alone, Sally said eagerly, ''It's all around the school about the new head.''

''I expect it is.''

Sally pulled a face of disappointment. ''You don't sound very interested.''

''Of course I'm interested,'' Helena said coolly. ''It's just that I'm submerged in work.''

Sally went over to search the bookshelf. ''Are you starting your homework?'' Helena asked.

''In a minute. I've something important to do first. It's awfully lucky you're a teacher. You've got so many useful books.'' She pulled down *Who's Who* and began to flick through its pages. ''Here we are. Bruce Venables—born November twenty-seven. That makes him Sagittarius.''

''Sally, I hardly think your new headmaster is a fit subject for your astrology predictions,'' Helena protested.

''Of course he is. Astrology applies to everyone in the whole world, everybody in the universe.''

Astrology was Sally's current hobby. No one was safe, not her teachers, her friends, or her favorite pop stars. She insisted on telling Helena what her stars predicted for her, despite receiving no encouragement to do so. Now she was in full flight. ''Do you know Sagittarius is the perfect sign for a teacher? Its symbol is the centaur, part horse, part man. In ancient mythology the centaur was the master of teaching and healing.'' She read aloud, '' 'Sagittarians are also known for their lack of diplomacy, and can be tactless and even unkind without meaning to be.' ''

''And sometimes with meaning to be,'' Helena said with feeling. Then she realized that she was talking as though she took this seriously, and checked herself. ''Don't waste time on it, Sally. It's all pointless.''

''How can you say that when the stars predicted a big change in your life this month? Getting a new headmaster is a big change, isn't it?''

''I...hardly think that counts,'' Helena said, taken aback. ''I'm sure it means something more personal.''

''But I heard you say once that the headmaster affects everybody for good or ill.''

''Well, yes...in a sense he does, but—'' She gathered her wits. ''You and I are right down at the bottom of the school, and he won't even notice us.''

''He'll notice you because you're so pretty,'' Sally said irrepressibly. ''I wish I looked like you, all tawny and magnificent.''

''What on earth do you mean, tawny?''

''Well, your hair being that color—tawny, like a lioness. It's so perfect, somehow, that your sign is Leo.''

''Get on with your homework,'' Helena said severely.

There was an air of suppressed excitement in the school next morning. Everyone suspected that the new head would arrive that day, although no one knew exactly when. Then, at midmorning break, the staff were summoned to the staff common room. Helena was delayed and hurried along, realizing she was going to be late. As she ran she phrased her apology.

But she needn't have worried. Bruce Venables was even later. Helena arrived to find the room packed with colleagues, most of them looking at their watches. "I wonder what's keeping him?" Alec, the senior history tutor, mused.

"Tactics. This is probably just his way of letting us know that his time is more important than ours," Helena declared.

There was a rumble of agreement. Helena wasn't the only one to think Bruce Venables had taken this job with indecent haste.

At that moment the door opened and a tall, dark-haired man swept into the room. Swept was the only possible word to describe it. He didn't seem to walk in the normal way, but arrived like a force of nature, setting the air vibrating. "Sorry everyone," he said cheerfully. "Didn't mean to keep you waiting, but I lost my way. No sense of direction. Never did have. I either lose things or barge into them."

His voice was an attractive baritone and his grin was infectious. The group seemed to relax simultaneously, and smiles began to appear.

"We'll have the proper introductions later," he went on, "but I thought I'd give you all a quick look at my face, so when you see me wandering around the school you won't think I'm an intruder and send for the law."

This time there was a definite laugh. In just a few seconds he was winning them over. All except Helena, who was holding in her mind a picture of poor George, lying in his hospital bed, while this interloper stole his school.

He began making his way around the staff while his secretary introduced him to each one by name. Helena had time to observe him, and realized that he was younger than she'd expected, not more than his mid-thirties, with dark, wavy hair, a lean face and laugh lines at the corners of his eyes. Oh yes, she thought crossly. Superficially he was very pleasant, and all the others were succumbing. He would find her a harder nut to crack. Someone had to be loyal to George.

Then it was her turn, and Bruce seized her hand and shook it firmly. His own hand was warm and strong, and she could feel her flesh tingle where his long fingers gripped it. As she looked up at him, the tingling seemed to spread until it encompassed her whole body. His eyes laughed directly into hers. They were dark brown, with a gleam that started far back in their depths, and they inspired her with an almost irresistible desire to smile at him in return. She mastered it. She wasn't going to abandon her principles so easily. With an effort she kept her face composed, greeting him politely, yet without yielding an inch.

But it was less easy to master her blood, which was suddenly racing in her veins, or her heart, which had begun to pound as he continued to hold her hand, cocking his head slightly with a quizzical air, as if to ask whether she wouldn't lighten up and give him the ghost of a smile. "It's a pleasure to meet you, Miss Walker," he said, and his deep attractive voice seemed to go through her.

"How do you do, Mr. Venables?" she said coolly.

"You're the form mistress for the second year students, aren't you?"

"That's right."

"Yes." He hesitated, as if he were wondering whether to say something else. And while Helena waited, he still had hold of her hand and she was thrillingly aware of his strong fingers gripping her dangerously close to her pulse with its mad racing.

Bruce's mind had the useful ability to work on several levels at once. It was doing so now, wondering why this young woman was looking at him with such frozen hostility, impervious even to his most winning smile. At the same time he was calculating whether or not to tell her something that would probably make her like him even less, and deciding that secret could wait awhile.

But these thoughts were superficial, using up barely one percent of his consciousness. The other ninety-nine percent was given over to pure, wide-eyed, open-mouthed, heart-thumping admiration. She was like a lioness with her tawny hair, warm skin and majestic bearing. Something disturbing was happening to him; something that shouldn't have happened for at least another few weeks. After all, he hadn't recovered from . . . from—well, whoever. The lady had walked out on him, declaring that he was absolutely impossible, an accusation he'd heard often before. He was devastated, heartbroken, disillusioned, and any minute now he would remember her name.

But not while this golden creature looked imperiously into his eyes and his heart looped the loop.

There was a discreet touch on his arm and he looked down to find the secretary ready to move him on. He came out of his dream to realize he'd probably made a spectacle of himself. He got through the rest of the introductions, hoping his self-consciousness didn't show, and soon as he could he thanked everybody and departed in a hurry.

Helena walked slowly back to her classroom, trying to organize her thoughts. She had a lesson to give, and normally she would have been running through her opening remarks as she walked, but suddenly her mind was a blank and her ears were filled with the music of the spheres. Still trying to steady herself, she opened the door and walked to the desk.

At once a boy detached himself from the crowd and approached her. "Good morning," he said politely.

"Good morning," she said mechanically, then looked at him more closely. "I think you've got the wrong class. I've never seen you before."

"You're Miss Walker?" he inquired.

"Yes."

"Then I'm in the right class. My name is Alastair Witton, and I'm new. I was told to report to you."

He spoke with the manner and precise English of a little old man, but he looked about eight. He wore large spectacles, and the eyes behind them were both innocent and strangely wise.

"No one told me you were coming, Alastair," she said, puzzled. "And I'm still not sure that this is the right place for you. How old are you?"

"I was ten last month."

"But everyone in this class is twelve. At ten you shouldn't even be in this school. You belong in the junior school down the road."

Alastair shook his head, his composure undisturbed. "I'm afraid I'm rather ahead of my age," he said, as if apologizing for some social error.

"Two years ahead?"

"Oh yes. You'll find that I keep up perfectly well. I may even need to go up another form, but my uncle felt I should start here until I settled in."

Helena resisted the temptation to clutch her head distractedly. "And just where does your uncle figure in the equation?" she inquired.

"He's Mr. Venables, the new headmaster."

Helena let out her breath slowly. "I see," she said. "But what about your parents? Didn't they have anything to say?"

"Well, Dad wasn't too sure, but Mom is Uncle Bruce's sister, and she said he knew best."

"I think I get the picture. Well, why don't you sit at that empty desk for the moment, and we'll talk later."

Unperturbed, Alastair took his seat at the desk next to Sally. Helena watched him with a smile, but inwardly she was seething.

As soon as the bell went for lunch she made straight for the headmaster's study. Bruce Venables looked up as she came in. "Sit down," he said. "Our lunch will be here in a moment."

"*Our* lunch?"

"Well, I had a feeling you'd be popping along. He's quite something when you first meet him, isn't he?"

"Mr. Venables—"

"Bruce, please."

"Mr. Venables, I appreciate that any relative of yours is bound to be brighter than average but don't you think you're allowing family partiality to run away with you?"

"To begin with, it doesn't follow that my relatives should be brighter than average," he replied mildly. "We have the usual percentage of clowns and screwballs, and since I come from a very large family, that adds up to an awful lot of clowns and screwballs. Do you come from a large family?''

Caught off guard by the unexpected question, she faltered. "I— No— I don't know— That is—"

He grinned. "How can you not know?"

"Can we stick to the point?"

"We've covered the first point. The second point is that I haven't let family partiality run away with me, because I never let personal feelings destroy my sense of proportion." Bruce was aware that this wasn't quite true where this young woman was concerned. Just the sight of her walking into his office had sent his sense of proportion into a state of gibbering collapse. But that was another matter.

"You send a ten-year-old boy into a class of twelve-year-olds and expect me to believe you haven't lost your sense of proportion?" Helena demanded. "Do you really think he'll be at home there?"

"Frankly, no. When he's got his bearings I imagine I'll probably have to move him up another year. Alastair's so brilliant that I'm constantly having to revise my opinion. But let's see how things work out, shall we? Ah, here's lunch."

The secretary wheeled in a trolley bearing chicken salad and crusty rolls. While she was in the room, Helena was obliged to keep quiet and it gave her time to think. It was astonishing to have discovered Bruce Venables' weakness so soon. Beneath his intellectual brilliance he was just another proud relative. And to think this man had had the nerve to accuse *her* of simplifying to the point of falsity.

When they were alone, Bruce said, "It looks good. Let's dig in."

"I'm afraid I can't stay," Helena said frostily. "I have some marking to do."

Bruce shook his head. "You shouldn't be marking during your lunch hour. It's bad for your digestion, and that's bad for your afternoon work. But we'll discuss your poor organization later."

He could have bitten his tongue off as soon as the last remark was out. It sounded patronizing and superior, and he hadn't meant it that way. But tactlessness was his middle name, and now he could see that he'd annoyed her further. She was getting up. "Sit down," he begged. "Have something to eat."

"I'd rather not, thank you. I think I should warn you, Mr. Venables, that I don't intend to stand by while you risk Alastair's well-being. If you won't be sensible, I'm prepared to take the matter higher."

Bruce's lips twitched. "But I'm the headmaster," he protested faintly. "Just how much higher do you think you can take it?"

"I can go to the school governors."

"What, the ones who twisted my arm to get me to take this job?" he asked with a grin. "Don't do it, Helena. It wouldn't add to your dignity."

She was dismayingly aware of that, but she went on firmly, "There is also the education authority. But before I try them I shall speak to the child's parents, whom I gather you bullied over this matter."

"Did Alastair say that?" Bruce asked with a grin.

"When I tell them how damaging it is to a child to be driven too hard simply to satisfy the aspirations of relatives—"

"Now you've gone too far," Bruce said, his humor vanishing. "I'm quite capable of satisfying my own aspirations without using a child. That's an outrageous accusation and I want you to withdraw it."

"I'll withdraw it when Alastair is in his proper place."

"Which, in my opinion, he already is."

"Then there's nothing more to say—for the present."

"There's nothing more to say at any time," Bruce said grimly. "I happen to be in charge here, and I don't intend to run to you for approval of my decisions. You can take that as final."

"I'll take his parents' word as final. Nothing else."

"Then I wish you luck in getting it, Miss Walker. Now please leave my office."

Helena departed in a flurry of tawny mane, leaving Bruce surveying the tête-à-tête lunch he'd planned so lovingly, and cursing his runaway tongue. With a little more diplomacy it might all have ended differently. But then, who'd ever heard of a diplomatic Sagittarian?

Chapter Two

Helena lost no time in securing Alastair's address, and headed for it that evening. It turned out to be in an apartment block that she knew to be much in demand, despite its shabby exterior.

Inside there was an air of old world charm. Even the lift seemed to belong to an earlier era, which made Helena pause nervously. As a child she'd had a bad experience with a malfunctioning lift, and to this day she had to fight with herself before she could get in one. But she refused to yield to her apprehension, and got inside. The ancient machine swayed and made mysterious noises, but its progress to the fifth floor was uninterrupted. Helena stepped out with relief and found herself facing the door of No. 37. It was opened as soon as she rang.

"Please come inside," Alastair said politely. "We've been expecting you."

Of course, Bruce had called them in advance. He might even have hurried over here to get his word in first. Well, she was prepared for battle.

"I'll take your coat," Alastair said. "Please sit down in there." He indicated a door off the hall.

Helena went through and found herself in a large room packed from floor to ceiling with books. Books stood on the desk, on the chairs, the mantelpiece. They bowed the shelves, they peeped out from under cushions, they supported ornaments, they turned the floor into an obstacle course.

In one corner stood a table covered with mathematical charts, plus the inevitable pile of books. Helena wandered over to look and discovered that the books were about astrology, but not the kind Sally studied. These were abstruse works full of complex calculations and incredibly detailed charts.

"Do you like them?" Helena turned to see Alastair carrying a tray into the room. He set it down and came to her. "It's my favorite hobby."

"This is all yours?"

"Yes. It's quite an art, you know. Are you at all interested in astrology?"

"No, but Sally is. She's the girl you were sitting next to today. We live in the same house."

"Does she do charts?"

"I don't think so. This would be a bit beyond her," Helena said, slightly dazed. "It's fascinating, Alastair, but—"

"I know. I'm sorry you're being kept waiting. It shouldn't be more than a moment or two. I've explained that you're here. In the meantime, I'm to look after you. Do you like sugar in your tea?"

"No, thank you. Shall I pour?"

"No, that's my job," the little boy responded with perfect self-possession. When he'd finished and she'd tasted the tea and found it perfect, he asked politely, "Would you mind telling me your birthday?"

"August twenty-third."

"Then you're a Leo. That's a fire sign, ruled by the sun."

"Yes, Sally told me."

"It's an excellent sign, warm-hearted and generous, and very noble. Uncle Bruce is Sagittarius, which is also a fire sign, but it's ruled by Jupiter, which can get a bit awkward. He's terribly wise and learned about some things, and quite thick about others. He's always running away from ladies."

"I beg your pardon?"

"From ladies. They want to marry him, but Sagittarians believe freedom is everything and Uncle Bruce says no one's going to get a noose around his—"

"That will do, thank you," Bruce said, appearing hastily in the door. "I'll take over the entertaining."

Alastair vanished and Bruce regarded Helena self-consciously. "I don't suppose I've got much character left," he said. "But I promise I'm not the Bluebeard he makes me out."

"Mr. Venables, there's no need for you to explain anything to me. I'm not in the least interested in your love life."

"I was afraid of that," he murmured so softly that she barely heard him.

"Can I see Alastair's parents now?" she asked, wondering if her ears had deceived her. "Or did you persuade them to leave before I got here?"

"I give you my word I haven't told them you're coming. But can you hang on a minute? My first day at Edenbrook was pretty hectic and I could do with someone to hold my hand.''

The words brought back the memory of his hand closed over hers that morning, holding it on and on, the fingers imprinting themselves on her flesh, and to her dismay her heart began to beat more strongly. Worse still, she could feel herself beginning to blush. "I'm sure you'll prove extremely competent once you're used to Edenbrook," she said coolly.

He regarded her quizzically. "You certainly know how to put a knife into a man's ego, don't you?" he said wryly.

"I'm not sure what—"

"Competent! Of all the insulting things to be called. If I thought I'd never rate better than 'competent' I'd put a pistol to my head now."

"I think you're making an absurd fuss over nothing," she said crisply. "If I'd called you *in*competent you could have complained, but competent is generally held to be a word of approval."

"And there lies the cleverness. While appearing to praise me you actually imply that I'm a lump who will never rise beyond mediocrity. Nice one! Acerbic but neat. I'm sure Alastair would be able to explain it to me in terms of your stars and planets."

"Alastair has already informed me that I'm a Leo," she couldn't stop herself saying.

"I find that hard to believe. Leo is a warm, outgoing sign, full of passion and generosity."

"I know nothing about it," she said, trying to halt his flow of words. "And I'm surprised to find a man of your intellect giving it a moment of your attention."

"But I thought we'd just agreed that my intellect was no more than competent," he said wickedly. He noticed how annoyance made the color come and go in her cheeks, and suddenly he found it possible to see her as a Leo after all. "Anyway, why shouldn't I give it my attention?" he went on, keeping his eyes on her face.

"Because it's hopelessly unscientific, as you well know."

"But I don't know. Nor do you. Nor does anyone. I don't accept it at face value, but I won't reject it until I've learned a great deal more." He quoted, " 'There are more things in heaven and earth, Horatio, than are dreamt of in your philosophy.' Who knows what there is in heaven and earth? Perhaps you really are a Leo, after all—warm, generous, and passionate?"

Something in the way he said "passionate" made her heart begin to thump hard. For some reason the word seemed overwhelmingly significant. She drew a deep breath and tried to force the conversation back onto its original track. "I can only repeat," she said, trying to keep her voice steady, "that you will soon get used to Edenbrook—"

"I won't. I never much cared for being a schoolmaster. I can't stand the routine."

"Indeed? And yet the governors of one of the best schools in the country were 'begging' you to take the job?" she reminded him.

He colored. "I didn't mean that to sound as conceited as it did. You just got under my skin. Can't we forget it and call a truce?"

"You won't put me off that easily. I'm here to see Alastair's parents and that's what I'm going to do if I have to stay here all night."

A gleam came into his eyes. "Well, if you're going to stay here all night, let me make you comfortable," he said, rearranging some cushions behind her back. The movement brought him close to her, his arm almost around her shoulders, his mouth within inches of hers. Helena forced herself to keep calm. This was going all wrong. She'd planned how tonight would go, but her calculations hadn't included finding herself alone with the most dangerously exciting male animal she'd ever met.

"I didn't mean that I was literally going to stay here," she said in a voice that she hoped didn't quaver. "Will you please stop stalling me and let me see Alastair's parents?"

"I'm afraid that will be rather difficult," he said, his eyes dancing.

"Why?"

"Because they're in Nigeria."

"What—*since when?*"

"I didn't pack them off there to avoid you, I swear it," he declared.

"You're quite capable of it," she said, seething.

"I don't know what I've done to get into your black books," he sighed. "You seem to think I'm a cross between Svengali and Attila the Hun. But in this case I'm completely innocent. My brother-in-law is a mining engineer working on a contract out there. The climate doesn't suit Alastair, so he's staying with me until they return, in about eight months' time."

"And of course, you couldn't just have told me that today?" she fumed.

"But you never asked me. Besides, you weren't interested in the facts if they got in the way of your prejudices. It's what I'm always warning Alastair about—the dangers of not doing some thorough preliminary research. He's got a great future in math if he can control his tendency to jump to conclusions."

"If I can control *mine,* you mean?" she said crossly. Inwardly she was furious because he was right. She could have discovered the situation from Alastair himself.

"I might mean that, too," he agreed. "Did you do any research? Did you test Alastair to discover what stage he's reached?"

"Well I—"

"No, you didn't. You said, 'Ten-year-old child—identical with all other ten-year-olds.' Whizz, bang!" He made a gesture of finality.

Helena sought for words, trying not to be put off by the mischievous twinkle in his eyes, and finally settled for the one accusation she could refute. "I certainly did not go 'whizz, bang!'" she declared.

"Your actions did. You couldn't wait to put him in a pigeon hole. You terrify me, Helena. You seem to see things in such terribly simple terms, but sometimes that leads to a kind of distortion."

Helena paled. "I'd better go."

Bruce stared. "Now, what have I said to offend you? It was an impartial comment. Besides, we haven't seriously discussed my nephew yet."

"But you aren't prepared to discuss him," Helena said scornfully. "'I'm in charge.' Those were your words this afternoon. Anyone who disagrees with you can just keep quiet."

Bruce groaned. "Don't remind me what I said. I'm ashamed of it. I'm always blurting things out and regretting it the next moment. Please stay, and let's talk."

She hesitated. She had no desire to stay after that remark about simplifying, which had come so perilously near the nerve, but she couldn't let Bruce suspect what his comment had meant to her. "I explained my point of view today," she said. "Despite your 'whizz, bang!' theories I don't think he'll be happy in a class of twelve-year-olds."

"You think he'll be happy with ten-year-olds? He wouldn't. He'd be bored out of his mind because he's mentally so far ahead of them. And a bored child is a danger to other people and himself, mostly himself. I know. I've been there. I was as precocious as Alastair, and I nearly went crazy because my teachers tried to keep me back to the pace of the others. I started doing things I shouldn't, just to pass the time."

"What sort of things?"

Bruce grinned. "Never mind. They got me expelled from one school and landed me in a juvenile court. It was just mischief, but I might have turned into a real delinquent. Luckily the woman who was on duty as counselor on my court day had a brother who was a teacher, and she told him about me. He got me into this school, and he let *me* set the pace. I'll always be grateful to that man. He saved my sanity."

His grin had faded, and when he spoke of his mentor a light came into his eyes. Now he seemed to emerge from a dream and pull himself up short, returning almost defiantly to the humorous mode. "He also did the world a favor. I'd have been a fine master criminal."

"You take it for granted that you'd have been a huge success?" she observed with cool irony.

"A success?" he echoed hilariously. "Of course I'd have been a success! The police of three continents would have been falling over their feet. By now I'd have a mansion in Mayfair, a pad in the south of France and twenty million in the bank. Instead, here I am, an underpaid schoolmaster."

"You'll have me crying in a minute," Helena said dryly.

"Well, like most people, I cherish the thought that I could have achieved more if I'd done certain things differently. Don't you have some moment in your life that you look back on wistfully, and think, 'But for that, things would be different today'?"

"Yes," Helena said, thinking of her book and its sorry end. "I do."

"Tell me about it," he coaxed, watching her face, fascinated by the different expressions that fleeted across it.

But Helena's reserve descended on her like a cloak. "We're not here to discuss my private affairs," she said primly, and he knew it would be useless to pursue the matter now. If only he could be alone with her in some private place, where he could wine her and dine her and coax out the secret that made her look like that.

"I don't mind admitting my mistakes," he conceded. "I'd be several rungs further up the ladder if I'd guarded my tongue a bit more."

She'd meant to maintain an attitude of indifference to his outpourings, but this goaded her into saying, "Guard your tongue? You?"

"I know, I know. It's been the bane of my life. Telling a man he's a pompous ass isn't usually wise, especially if it's true."

"You mean people are actually so unreasonable as to object to the unkind things you say about them?"

"Not unkind. Truthful."

"Well, there are many ways of phrasing criticism without being cruel."

"I don't believe I'm ever cruel," he said seriously. "Certainly I don't set out to be." He spoke abstractedly because something in her manner struck him as strange. It was almost as though she wasn't talking to him at all, but to some unseen third presence. He studied her face for a clue to the mystery, and discovered that at close quarters she was even more stunning than he'd realized. Her mouth was wide and curved, and the contrast between it and the prim words that issued from it intrigued him. He wondered how that mouth would kiss. Would it be prim or generous? And how soon could he find out?

"Mr. Venables, are you listening to me?"

"I beg your pardon?" he said, coming quickly out of his reverie. "Did you say something?"

"I said I hope you don't talk this way to Alastair."

"I talk to Alastair about anything he wants to talk about."

"Including the ladies that you're always having to run away from," Helena couldn't resist retorting. For some reason that had nettled her.

Bruce colored, but managed to grin. "That's disappointment speaking. Alastair is trying to marry me off so that he can have a change from my cooking. Actually, I'm not as bad as he makes out. Why don't you stay and form your own opinion?"

"I'm afraid that's impossible. I have to go."

"Why?" A disturbing thought came to him. "You don't have someone's supper to cook, do you?"

"Yes," she said firmly, and his heart sank, only to rise again when she added, "my own."

"I meant someone else," he hinted.

"I'm not caring for an elderly parent if that's what you're getting at."

Was she tormenting him on purpose? he wondered. "No, I meant, someone *else*. A man."

"I'm unmarried. You know that from my file."

"I haven't had time to read your file—"

"You mean you didn't prepare for this battle with a little preliminary research? How careless of you."

He grinned. "Touché. Anyway, there might still be a man. Being unmarried doesn't mean a lot these days."

He made this last observation with one eyebrow raised inquiringly, which gave his face an unsettling quirky quality that she tried to ignore. "To some people, possibly," she responded coolly. "But I assure you the school won't get touched with scandal through me." An exasperated little devil made her add, "I'm not so sure about you."

At once she wished she hadn't said it, for somehow the devil was sitting in his eyes, teasing her, and making him say, "You mean you *are* sure, don't you?"

It was alarming what his smile could do to her insides. She disapproved of him on principle, but principle seemed of very little account right this minute. She had an intense awareness of danger. It was nothing like the danger that frightened her in lifts. In fact there was no fear at all, only a thrilling sense that the world was rocketing out of control, and that she liked it. Somehow her fragmented wits found George's name and clung to it. George, who'd been betrayed; George, whom she must defend, and not go weak at the knees because this man had a warm, wicked smile that began in his dark brown eyes and only seemed to reach his mouth as an afterthought. That thought made her look at his mouth, and she regretted it at once because she was riveted by the curve of the wide lips and the imp of mischief that lurked in the corner. *George. Help!*

"I see no point in continuing this discussion," she declared, summoning all her resolve.

"But there's every point," he insisted. "I have to get to know my staff—"

"Then I suggest that you consult my file at school," Helena said. She knew she sounded brusque but she couldn't help it. She had to escape.

"But I— Hey, don't go!" He leapt to his feet and hurried after her. "You can't just leave like this," he insisted as they reached the front door.

"I can."

She was out in the corridor. Bruce caught up with her with one long stride and seized her hands. "Look, I'm sorry for whatever I did—or said—or . . . or whatever. Let's go back and talk about it."

His closeness was treacherously enjoyable. At the corner of her consciousness she was vaguely aware that the lift had arrived and someone had stepped out. She stood with her hands in his, flesh tingling with delight, principle warring with pleasure.

But then Bruce overreached himself. With a flirtatious movement that was suspiciously practiced, he drew one of her hands up and brushed his lips against it. "Suppose we—" he started to say.

But before he could finish, Helena had wrenched herself free, darted into the open lift and pressed the button to go down. Bruce reacted like lightning, getting into the lift barely half a second behind her and pressing the first button he came to.

The conflict of the instructions was too much for the elderly machinery. The door closed. The lift swayed down half a floor and came to a shuddering halt.

Chapter Three

The jerky movement sent Helena toppling off-balance, straight into Bruce's arms. He steadied her against his chest, looking down with pleasure into her face. To his delighted surprise a change had come over her. Her cheeks were flushed, her lips trembled and he could feel the thundering of her heart close to his own. Scarcely knowing what he did, except that it felt natural and completely right, Bruce lowered his head and kissed her.

He felt her gasp against his lips, and sensed the pounding of her heart grow more wild. So the prim Miss Walker was a true, passionate Leo after all, he thought, and that was wonderful. He intensified the kiss, holding her slim body against his own, enjoying the feel of her trembling.

He was a practiced flirt, but at once he realized that this kiss was different. The knowledge came creeping through his senses as a joyous revelation, sending a fountain of delight shooting up through him. The future was a mystery, but his instincts told him that she had the power to blot out all other women from his consciousness. There was honey and wine on her lips and sweet perfume in her breath. He felt transported to another world, one where every breeze was gentle and every dream could be fulfilled. But there was only one dream, *this* new dream here in his arms, melting and tantalizing him in the same moment, seeming to yield, yet holding back something precious whose sweet allure enticed him on....

But then part of him that had held onto sensitivity through a lifetime of too much easy success, an instinct that he couldn't have named but which was decent and generous, warned him that he'd gotten everything horribly wrong. He drew back quickly, looking down. And now the trembling of her mouth and the little gasps that came from it looked less like passion than fear, and suddenly he was swept by remorse. "I'm sorry," he said quickly. "I didn't mean— I never thought— You're scared, aren't you?"

"No," she declared with an attempt at firmness that came out shakily. "Of course I'm not scared. Let me go at once."

He released her, but in the same moment the lift gave another jerk and fell three feet. This time Helena couldn't contain the cry that broke from her, but she managed not to fall against him, holding grimly onto the wall.

Bruce fought down the instinct to take hold of her, even to offer comfort. Every nerve in his body was tingling, but he knew if he came on strong while she was trapped with him he'd kill his chances—such as they were. To have held the beautiful dream in his arms and have it snatched away made him ache with deprivation, but he gritted his teeth and thought only of her. "It's all right," he said, trying to reassure her. "This lift is a bit temperamental but there's nothing wrong with the cable, I promise you." When she didn't reply, he said sympathetically, "I ought to be shot, acting like that."

"Yes," she replied, not mincing matters.

"I'll keep my distance from now on."

"You make it sound as if we were going to be here a long time," she said in a voice of such despair that his heart did a painful somersault.

"No, I won't let that happen," he declared. He took a deep breath and roared, *"Alastair."* He had to yell a few more times, but at last they heard the boy's voice. "Is that you, Uncle Bruce?"

"Yes. Call the porter and tell him this lift is stuck and he's to get someone here pronto." When Alastair had scampered away, Bruce said, "It shouldn't be long now. I'm afraid there's nowhere to sit."

"I'm perfectly all right, thank you."

"Look, Helena, I know it's too late for apologies, but I'm really sorry. I had no idea you were afraid of lifts."

"I am not afraid of lifts," she said emphatically. "I came up in this lift and it was fine. It would have been fine going down if you hadn't acted like a crazy man and jammed the works."

"Yes. I'm afraid I'm like that. I act first and think afterward. Not a very good recommendation for a headmaster, and I dare say I'm not most people's idea of what a headmaster should be. I know I'm not yours. You've disliked me from the first moment, and

I have to admit I seem to have confirmed your worst fears, but—"

He was talking on automatic, saying anything and everything that came into his head, trying to hold her attention so that she had something to distract her from her fear. He wished she would confide in him, but he knew he had no right to expect it. Her face was pale and set, telling him that she was fighting some inner battle, but fighting it alone.

At last the words ran out. She made some light, meaningless reply, but he could tell it was an effort. Her misery hurt him, and her gallant efforts to hide it hurt even more.

At last there was the welcome sound of engineers shouting from above, and a few minutes' later the lift shuddered again. He resisted the temptation to steady her, and luckily, after that first jerky movement, the lift steadied and went smoothly to the ground.

As Helena stepped out Bruce could see that she was shaking in every limb, although her head was high. He followed her determinedly to where her car was parked, and waited until she'd unlocked it. "I'm going to drive you home," he said.

"Thank you, but—"

"I'm going to drive you home," he interrupted firmly. "You'd have an accident if you tried to drive in the state you're in. Don't worry. I'm strictly the chauffeur, nothing more. Get in the back seat."

She made no further resistance, gave him the address, and then sat in silence for the rest of the way. From time to time he glanced at her face in the rearview mirror. She looked pale and exhausted.

The address turned out to be a piece of wasteland being used as a parking lot. When they'd gotten out of the car and he'd returned her key, he said, "Where do you live? It looks like the middle of nowhere."

"In one of those houses," she said, pointing. "This is just the easiest place to park. How will you get home?"

"There's a phone booth over there. I'll call a cab. Shall I walk you to the door?"

"Thank you, but—I'm fine now. I really am. Goodnight, Mr. Venables."

She turned quickly and walked away. Bruce watched her until she'd vanished into the darkness, wondering in which of the houses she lived. When the last echo of her footsteps had died away he went to the phone booth and thrust his hand into his pocket for change.

Then he realized he'd rushed out without any money.

His first instinct was to dash in the direction he'd seen Helena leave, but she was out of sight. She'd gone into one of those houses, but he had no way of knowing which one. He was in an unfamiliar part of London, miles from home.

Luckily the stars shone brightly, and by their guidance he managed to work out which direction was north. He began the long trudge home, but soon the hard pavement seemed to vanish and there were only flowers around him, dancing and nodding about his feet, filling the air with perfume. He was remembering how Miss Walker had felt, and the moment of passionate response that had thrilled him before the whole dream had disintegrated.

Had she responded? Before fear had overcome her, hadn't there been one glorious moment when she'd forgotten everything but being in his arms, and given back passion for passion?

The stars swung above him, cold and indifferent; or perhaps compassionate and knowing. Who could tell? He stopped and looked up at them.

"She *did* kiss me back," he informed them defiantly. "Yes she did. And what's more, I'm going to make sure she does it again."

At about 2:00 a.m. Alastair closed the book he'd been reading under the bedclothes, and lay for a moment in thoughtful silence. Then he slipped out of bed, left the room and made his way quietly to his uncle's room. When his tap was answered by a grunt, he pushed the door gently open and looked inside. The room was dark but for a glimmer of moonlight that showed him the shape of Bruce's head on the pillow. "Uncle," he whispered.

There was another grunt.

"I've just made the most astounding discovery. Do you want to hear it?" Taking the mumbled response for acquiescence, Alastair hurried on eagerly, "I've been checking the charts of compatibility, and I've found that Sagittarius and Leo are the most perfect combination in the whole universe. Can you believe that?

"It's a bit strange that Miss Walker doesn't like you, because you're Sagittarius and she's Leo, and that's dynamite. But perhaps she's trying to fight it. Do you think so?"

This time the mumble resolved itself into something like words. "I think . . . go back . . . bed . . . know what's good for you . . ."

Alastair frowned. "Perhaps you're right," he said at last. "On second thought, I believe a little more preliminary research is called for."

He slipped out, closing the door quietly behind him.

In the early hours Bruce awoke with a strange feeling. Somewhere during the night he'd had a dream. He couldn't remember the details, except that it had contained a warning or a prediction, he wasn't sure which. The words "Sagittarius" and "Leo" floated through his brain. Perhaps he'd been dreaming about astrology. But what?

There'd been another dream, too. In it, Miss Walker had smiled and opened her arms to him, and it had been wonderful. He'd held her, feeling her beautiful lioness hair stream over his hands, their faces drawing closer together. But at the last moment she'd pulled herself free and fled him.

He groaned, remembering the events of the evening. He'd had to walk three miles before he'd found a police station where a sympathetic desk sergeant had called a cab for him. But it was his own behavior that discomfitted him most of all.

You fool! he reflected. You imbecile, you self-centered, inconsiderate, selfish, moronic *jerk*. You thought you had only to come on strong and she would melt, didn't you? And all that happened was that you gave her nightmares. Serve you right if you had a long walk.

But the other memory couldn't be entirely banished. The beating of her heart and the flutter of her lips beneath his—that hadn't all been panic? Surely?

He tried to settle back to sleep, but something was nagging at him—part of his dream.

Yes, that was it. There'd been a disembodied voice warning—or was it encouraging?—him about Sagittarius and Leo. *She* was Leo.

It would have been simple to seek guidance from his precocious nephew, but for some reason he balked at that. He must work this one out alone. But there was a book that might help him. It was called *Heavenly Conjunctions* and he'd seen it in Alastair's possession.

A noise in the corridor informed him that Alastair was making his way sleepily to the bathroom. Bruce wasted no time wrestling with his conscience, but sprinted into the little boy's room. By a lucky chance *Heavenly Conjunctions* was lying in plain sight on the bedside table. He seized it up, escaped and went to the kitchen. There he made himself a large pot of black coffee, which he took to his room. Thus fortified, he consulted the book.

There it was: Sagittarius and Leo, the most heavenly conjunction of them all. Two signs that the stars seemed to have created especially for each other. Their compatibility was perfect in all areas, friendship, romance—and marriage. That made him swallow some coffee hastily, for marriage was as far from his thoughts as it had ever been in the course of his colorful youth. But the book assured him that when Miss Leo discovered his need for freedom she would respond with warm, generous understanding.

He cast his mind back to Helena's remark about "the ladies you're always having to run away from." He couldn't honestly say that warm, generous understanding had been uppermost in her voice at that moment. But that was Alastair's fault. The little wretch's gabbiness had spoiled his chances.

His alarm clock shrieked, startling him, so that he jumped with the cup halfway to his lips and had to dab frantically at spilled coffee. With a shock, he realized what he'd been doing. He was, as he'd told Helena, open-minded about astrology, as about most things, but he still inclined to the side of skepticism. Yet he'd spent the best part of an hour brooding on their astrological compatibility. True, the thought of any sort of compatibility with the ravishing Helena sent hot shivers scurrying over his skin....

At that moment he heard Alastair's bedroom door open, and his footsteps make another advance toward the bathroom. It was the work of a moment to return the book and slip back to his own room without, thank goodness, Alastair suspecting a thing.

There's no surer path to friendship than shared obsession, and it took only a few minutes for Sally and Alastair to become bosom buddies.

"I feel very responsible for Uncle Bruce," Alastair explained while Sally nodded gravely. "I was sure he was awake, but it's clear now that he wasn't."

"Then how do you know that he heard you?" Sally wanted to know.

"Because of the way he's acting. In the early hours of this morning he secretly borrowed my copy of *Heavenly Conjunctions* and returned it without saying anything. He thinks I didn't notice, but naturally I did. For one thing, there was a coffee stain in a highly significant place, which wasn't there when I was reading it last night."

"A *highly significant* place?" Sally breathed.

"Right in the middle of the chapter about Sagittarius and Leo," Alastair declared in a solemn voice. "I brought it with me. Look." Alastair produced the book and showed Sally the page, which she viewed with reverence. "And at breakfast this morning he kept leading the subject around to astrology, under the guise of taking an interest in my hobbies. He heard what I said last night, but only in his sleep, and now he thinks it's his own idea.''

"But surely that's good? He's more likely to listen to his own ideas than yours. Grown-ups are funny that way.''

Alastair nodded. "I agree. Totally unreasonable. No sense of logic whatever. It *is* a good thing, providing that I'm right in my original assessment.''

"But how could you be wrong?'' Sally queried with an unconscious emphasis on "you'' that made Alastair regard her with favor.

"Not exactly wrong,'' he conceded. "More like, superficial. After all, every Sagittarius isn't right for every Leo. A lot depends on what the planets were doing at the moment they were born, and for that you need the year, and the exact time, if possible. I can get that for Uncle Bruce, but I need Miss Walker's details.''

"I'll see what I can do,'' Sally promised.

Alastair nodded owlishly. "Good. It's especially important with her, because she was born on the last day before Leo becomes Virgo, which means she's on the cusp, and may have some Virgo tendencies.''

"And suppose you discover that they really are perfect for each other? What are you going to do?''

"Promote the match as hard as possible, of course. I don't want to see Uncle Bruce end up a lonely old man because his Sagittarian love of freedom got out of hand.''

Sally nodded. "It's really your duty to help him, isn't it?"

"Of course it is. Besides, I need an aunt. His cooking's terrible."

Chapter Four

By watching carefully for the right moment, Bruce managed to catch up with Helena in a natural way as she was going downstairs in the main school building. "How are you feeling today?" he asked.

"I'm fine, thank you," she said cheerfully. But her pale face told another story. She looked as if she'd hardly slept the night before. "Did you get home all right?" she asked politely.

It was on the tip of his tongue to say mechanically "Fine. No problem," following the habit of a lifetime in which it had become necessary to make effortless success seem the norm. It had started long ago when he'd been the golden boy who always came top of the class and carried off the school prizes. His family's innocent pride had urged him on to more achievement, and from there to a denial of even the tiniest failure. For Bruce Venables, taxis always arrived and gas never ran out—except when he wanted it to. He might have become obnoxious but for a kind heart and a sense of humor that kept him on an even balance. But the habit of smoothing over the cracks had persisted, making him now instinctively ready to claim that everything had gone as he wished.

But he stopped himself, because it dawned on him that the true story might give her pleasure, might even make her smile. It would be worth the sacrifice of his pride to banish that look of strain from her face. "Eventually," he said with a self-mocking smile. "When I reached the phone booth I found I'd come out without any money, so I couldn't even call a cab. It was too late to ask to use your phone. You were already out of sight."

"You mean you had to walk all the way home?" she asked, aghast.

"Not quite. I found a police station and they let me call from there. But I had to walk three miles first. I'm telling you this so that you'll know I got my just desserts. I'm sure that will please you."

She managed a smile. "That would be pretty mean of me, wouldn't it?"

And the lion is a noble beast, he thought, *incapable of pettiness.*

"Helena," he said impulsively, "do you have anyone to talk to—any close family, for instance?"

"Why?"

"Because you look as if you need to talk and get whatever's troubling you out of your system."

"There's nothing—"

"Don't pretend," he pleaded. "You were terrified in that lift last night—and I don't just mean of me."

"I certainly wasn't terrified of you," she asserted with a lift of her head that made him wish she were wearing her hair loose this morning. How her lovely mane would have swirled with that movement. But it was pinned back neatly, and he could only dream. "Don't bottle things up," he urged. "It's dangerous."

"Sure. I'll find someone."

She was about to turn away from him. He made an impulsive decision. "Look, you'll probably think it's outrageous of me to even suggest such a thing, but why not talk to me? After all," he hurried on quickly before she could reply, "I start with the advantage of being halfway there. I know what your problem is—or part of it, anyway. And I'm a very good listener."

"I expect you are, but surely you can see that—"

"I'd promise to behave myself. It'll be like talking to a brother, and you'll feel better afterward."

"Well . . ." She stopped, torn by indecision.

"Won't you give me a chance to atone?"

"Mr. Venables—"

"Bruce."

"Bruce, you're making a mountain out of a mole-hill. I've fought off unwanted passes before."

He winced at that "unwanted" but said only, "This wasn't just a pass. I did something that gave you nightmares. Please, give me a chance to pay my debts."

She smiled suddenly and he caught his breath. "All right. We'll talk sometime."

"Not 'sometime'. Tonight."

"I can't make it directly after school," she said, thinking of Sally.

"Neither can I," he said. "I have something to do first. I'll collect you at your home at eight-thirty. I have your full address now.'' He grinned cheekily. ''I checked your file this morning.''

''Are you sure it's a good idea to—''

''Eight-thirty,'' he repeated firmly, and strode off without giving her a chance to protest further.

The minute he was out of sight, Helena regretted her rash decision. She was on the verge of chasing him and canceling the arrangement, but the impulse died. She did need to talk. Bruce had read that signal correctly. But to him? Wasn't it crazy to turn to the author of all her troubles? Then she knew it was no use pondering the matter. Bruce wouldn't take no for an answer and that was that.

There would be no problem about Sally. Mrs. Carter always returned from the hospital by eight-thirty. The child had arrived after dinner and settled at the table with her books. But she seemed distracted, and every now and then Helena felt she was about to say something.

''What is it, Sally?'' she asked at last.

''Nothing, Miss Walker,'' Sally said hastily. ''It's just—''

''Yes?''

''In history, you were expected to be grown up when you were twelve, weren't you? I mean, lots of girls got married at twelve.''

''Sometimes. If they were rich their families married them off to the sons of other rich families, and they didn't have any choice. Poor people often didn't live past thirty-five, so they had to grow up fast.''

''So if this were the thirteenth century, I'd be grown up and you'd be terribly old?''

"If this were the thirteenth century you wouldn't be sitting here in a nice warm room, full of tea and fish-cakes," Helena pointed out, amused. "You'd be feeding the pigs and hurrying to get to bed before dark. And I wouldn't be old. I'd be middle-aged."

"How old is that?" Sally ventured.

Helena laughed. "Get on with your homework. I'm not telling you how old I am."

Sally sighed, accepting defeat, and returned to her books. Helena went into the bathroom and got into the shower. As she twisted under the water jet she pondered what to wear. Certainly it would be nothing glamorous. This mustn't be confused with a date. But hard on the heels of that thought came the memory of his arms closing around her in the lift, his mouth covering hers, and her body's treacherous response. For a wild moment her blood had raced in her veins, her heart had pounded and fire had streaked through her. No kiss had ever been so thrilling or evoked such a response from her. She'd wanted it to go on forever and ever, and while she felt like that she'd forgotten about the lift.

But then sanity had returned, and with it, her fear. She'd come reluctantly back to the real world, and found it a hard place, one where she didn't want to be. It had been an effort to jump-start her conscience into remembering George, but she had done her duty and withdrawn from Bruce.

She'd resolved to have nothing further to do with this dangerous man, but then he'd proved again just how dangerous he was, luring her into this meeting— *not* date—by giving her a sense of security, talking of being brotherly. How come she'd fallen for it?

There would be just time to call and put him off. Stepping out of the shower she pulled on a terry-cloth robe and went into the living room. Sally was engrossed in a book, but it wasn't a schoolbook. "Sally, surely you haven't been spending your pocket money on more astrology books?" Helena chided. She glanced over the child's shoulder. "And that one looks really expensive."

"It's all right, Miss Walker, I didn't buy it. Alastair lent it to me."

"And you're going to give it back to him with that coffee stain all over it?"

"It was already like that," Sally protested.

Helena touched the page gingerly. "It's still damp," she pointed out.

"Alastair said his uncle did that early this morning."

"Do you really expect me to believe that?"

"No, honestly, Alastair said his uncle borrowed this before breakfast and sneaked it back again without saying anything." Sally stopped suddenly, as if aware of having revealed too much. But Helena's thoughts had taken another turn.

"Mr. Venables is your headmaster, Sally. He doesn't 'sneak.'"

Except that he snuck George's job, said her inner voice. *Don't forget that.*

Without further delay she dialed Bruce's apartment, turning her back and lowering her voice so that Sally couldn't hear. The phone was answered by Alastair. "I'm afraid Uncle Bruce isn't here," he said in answer to her query. "He's gone out for the evening. Can I give him a message?"

"No, there's no message."

"Can I say who called?"

"Er, nobody," Helena said quickly. "It doesn't matter." She hung up quickly, hoping Alastair hadn't recognized her voice. She didn't want to become an object of school gossip.

She returned to her room and surveyed her wardrobe with dissatisfaction. Her clothes were either chosen to be severe for school or stylish for going out. There was nothing that caught exactly the mood she was after, casually elegant but firmly unapproachable. On second thought she decided it would be better to look severe, and donned the same dark gray skirt and high-necked blouse that she'd worn for school that day. They made her point perfectly, she felt.

Sally regarded her in silence as she emerged from the bedroom, then vanished downstairs. She returned a moment later with a perfume spray, and got determinedly to work.

"*Sally*—stop it! What are you doing?" Helena cried, trying to dodge away from the musky perfume that filled the air.

"I'm sorry, Miss Walker, I didn't expect it to be so strong."

"But what is it? Where did you get it?"

"It's Mum's. Uncle John brought it back from Paris last time he was there. He said she needed some sparkle in her life. I thought it would give you a bit of sparkle for your date."

"It's not a date, Sally," Helena said. "It's more like a...like an educational conference with a fellow teacher." She didn't mention the teacher's identity, and it didn't occur to her that Sally might already know. She took the spray from Sally and groaned when she saw the name. "I can't go out smelling of *L'Eternité d'Amour,*" she said frantically.

"But it's good perfume, honestly. Uncle John said it was fifty pounds an ounce. And Mum never uses it."

Helena thought of her solidly respectable landlady and could believe it. This was a coquette's perfume. Only a kindly but naive brother would have bought it for prosaic Mrs. Carter. Only a daring woman would wear it, and then only the merest trace. And now she was covered in it.

"It was a nice thought, Sally, but it's not my style. I'll have to get out of these clothes. Put the perfume back where you found it."

Sally vanished. Helena tore off her clothes and scrubbed her skin vigorously, trying to remove every trace of the perfume. In despair she remembered that her other high-necked blouse was in the wash. She was quickly running out of time. Perhaps if she wore something stylish but black it would create the right ambience.

She had a black cocktail dress that had just come back from the cleaners. Hurriedly she took it off the rail and put it on, but at once she realized something was wrong. The dress had shrunk by a good deal, and instead of being subtly molded, it now hugged her curves in a way that could only be called suggestive. The neckline, which had once been slightly daring, now plunged dramatically, and the skirt revealed two inches more thigh than she would dream of showing.

So much for the right ambience, she thought. The ambience was hopeless. It would have to be slacks and a sweater.

But immediately there was a knock on her bedroom door and Sally looked in without waiting for an answer. "Your date has arrived," she said, pushing the door wide. "He rang the bell while I was downstairs, so I brought him up."

Helena opened her mouth to insist yet again that this wasn't a date, but before she could speak she heard the longest and most appreciative wolf whistle of her life. Bruce was standing behind Sally looking into the bedroom and taking in the picture Helena presented.

She didn't notice Sally scuttling away. She was in turmoil over this development. Bruce was regarding her with deep, silent appreciation. A smile just touched his lips, and there was a look in his eyes that made a warmth start in her loins and creep upward until it engulfed her madly beating heart. She took an unsteady breath as she tried to summon the words to order him out of her bedroom while she changed into something more suitable. But somehow the words got muddled and came out as a breathless, "You like it?"

"I think you look ravishing," he said simply, and there was a vibrant note in his voice that settled the matter. There was no way she was going to change out of a dress that could make this wickedly attractive man look at her like that, and sound like that.

"But it's not quite complete," he said thoughtfully.

"Isn't it?" she echoed, dazed.

"No, it needs something—here." He touched her neck lightly and a tremor went through her. "Do you have a necklace?"

"Only this." She opened a drawer in her dressing table and took out a little silver pendant.

"That's perfect. Let me put it on for you."

He took it from her, swiveled her around and draped the pendant about her neck. She could feel his fingertips lightly touching the nape of her neck, making her come singingly alive all over her body.

Bruce felt her tremors communicate themselves to him through his fingers and the warmth of her nearness, and his senses reeled. He'd promised her a brotherly evening and that had been what she'd seemed to want. But then he'd arrived to find her in this enticing garment that cried aloud for him to "come hither." Better still, as he leaned near to her he could detect the faintest possible traces of a musky and very seductive perfume.

His view of Miss Walker took yet another whirl. Was there no end to her secrets? He'd half expected lavender water, but she'd surprised him. A woman who could choose *L'Eternité d'Amour* knew a lot about men and how to entice them. What was more, she understood exactly how it should be worn for maximum effect, very sparingly, to thrill a man with elusiveness and mystery. He hated to have his senses blasted with an overdose of strong perfume, but this lady was a mistress of allure. She had him thoroughly confused, but it was a confusion that he liked.

"If you're ready, we could go," he said, offering her his arm.

Slightly dazed, Helena took it and let him lead her out of the bedroom. Sally was in the other room, her face full of blank innocence that Helena would have found suspicious if she'd been more alert. "I'll just tidy my things and go, Miss Walker," Sally said.

"Thank you, Sally. Goodnight."

Sally listened while they went downstairs and out the front door. From the window she watched as they got into Bruce's car and drove away. Then she went to the telephone and dialed Alastair's number.

Bruce's car didn't suggest an academic. It was a sleek, beautiful sports car, the vehicle of a man who lived and played both hard and fast. But then, Helena reflected, nothing about Bruce was typically academic, starting with the clear-cut, handsome profile that he was presenting to her now. He had the body of an athlete, taut, lean and muscular, and the look of a man who enjoyed active outdoor pursuits. Meeting him for the first time Helena might have thought he was a runner or a horse rider, but she wouldn't have associated him with the piles of books she'd seen at his home. His hands were particularly fine. The long, blunt-tipped fingers resting on the steering wheel suggested controlled power. She suddenly remembered how firmly and easily they had held her in the lift, and was glad that the fading light hid the way the blood rushed to her cheeks.

Bruce drove as if the car was a part of himself, threading his way through the London traffic with ease, until at last Helena saw that they'd reached the West End, a glamorous part of town that she seldom visited. "I...hadn't realized that we were coming here," she said.

Bruce hadn't planned it that way, either. He'd been thinking of a sedate restaurant, but had abandoned that idea the moment he'd encountered her in the low-cut black dress, wafting the fragrance of seduction. But he didn't answer her directly, just shrugged and said, "I thought we'd have a drink first."

He finally settled on a small bar where he knew they could have a booth, and privacy. He wasn't jealous by nature. A man who played the field as extensively as he did couldn't afford to be. But as they walked in and every male head turned toward them—to be precise, toward *her*—he knew an unaccustomed surge of possessiveness. He steered her to the booth as quickly as possible, anxious to get her to himself.

"What's happening to Alastair tonight?" she asked.

"I've got company for him. I don't say 'baby-sitter' for fear of Alastair's displeasure."

"I can imagine. After only two days I realize he's ten going on a hundred." She took a deep breath and said, "I asked him some really hard questions this morning, and he reeled off the answers as if he'd known them all his life. I have to admit you were right."

"That's very generous of you," he said, grinning.

"But I'm still a little concerned about his overall welfare. He could easily get bullied. I'm going to stay alert for that."

"Thank you. But I don't think you'll have much to do. Alastair has his own way with bullies. He fixes them with his dragon eye and warns them to be careful because Jupiter is rising in their seventh house. It usually sends them running for cover."

"You were teasing me the other night—weren't you?—about taking this astrology seriously."

His face wore a slightly puzzled frown. "That wasn't the other night, Helena. That was last night. We only met yesterday morning."

"Goodness, so we did. I lost track. It's just that—" She stopped.

But Bruce seemed to understand without being told. "Yes," he said nodding. "So much has happened. I can hardly believe it's only a few hours, either. The

question is, which starting point do we choose tonight?''

''I'm . . . not sure what you mean?''

''Do we go on from where we are, or from where we
would normally be after thirty-six hours' acquaintance?''

It was on the tip of her tongue to say that she wasn't
sure they had a choice, but her innate caution restrained her. ''Perhaps it's best to go slowly,'' she said.
''Thirty-six hours isn't a long time.''

It can be, he thought. *So can thirty-six minutes—or
seconds.*

But aloud he said simply, ''You're right.''

A waiter appeared to take their drink orders. Helena settled for a modest sherry. To her surprise Bruce
drank fruit juice. ''I'm driving,'' he explained.

Besides which his head was already reeling from the
effect she had on him, and a man could only take so
much. He wondered why she'd done her hair up, as
she wore it at school. It showed off her long, slender
neck, which he enjoyed, but still he longed to pull out
the pins and feel its soft beauty streaming over his
hands.

Deep inside him a voice was whispering, *This is going to be one wonderful evening.* He knew that voice.
It had always spoken to him when the rich fruit was
about to fall into his eager hands.

But this time there was another voice, one he'd
never heard before. It said, *A wonderful evening, sure.
But not the kind you wanted.*

He tried to tell it to shut up. Two voices were too
much to cope with. And as long as the evening worked
out well, did it matter why?

Yes, whispered the voice, refusing to shut up. *It matters because you thought this woman was different—sweet and natural, a lady with character as well as beauty. Now she's gone glossy and glamorous on you, and that makes her just like too many others.*

So who cares?

You care. Because she may not be special after all. And that's very sad. Admit it. You're secretly disappointed.

Get lost!

But you are, aren't you?

I said, get lost!

Chapter Five

Helena had the strangest sensation of floating outside herself. She could see Bruce clearly, but she could also see the gorgeous creature sitting near him, looking into his eyes and smiling. She was glamorous in a way that Helena had always thought was alien to herself. Her dress was outrageous, too low in the bosom, too high in the leg and too tight everywhere. It took courage to wear a dress like that, but this woman had all the courage and confidence in the world.

Every movement she made was practiced and controlled, nothing was spontaneous. She knew that the man was riveted by her, and she was determined to keep him that way. When she ate an olive she didn't just put it in her mouth as she would normally have done. She let her lips enclose it slowly, provocatively, so that he had time to consider what beautiful lips they were, and what magic they could work. When she laughed she let her head fall back a little, giving him a perfect view of her long white neck.

She had her reward. He was transfixed. His eyes never left her, and all the time they held a look—such a look. She'd never seen it any man's eyes before, but its meaning was unmistakable. He'd lost all consciousness of everything but her, and the knowledge sent her flying high as a kite.

She was witty, too. Scintillating, frothy conversation tripped off her tongue, making him laugh. The time sped past. Somehow they'd been here an hour. She couldn't remember anything either of them had said.

Bruce, parrying her remarks with similar ones, equally meaningless, felt two opposing reactions pulling him apart. There was disappointment because he'd really wanted to get to know Helena this evening, but she'd vanished behind this glittering facade, and there was no reaching her. On the other hand—his eyes drifted down her plunging neckline—and further hand, to where her hips flared. Something seemed to be constricting his breathing.

He wondered what was the matter with him. In the past, to have a desirable woman putting herself out to entertain him would have been more than enough. But suddenly he wanted more. He tried to pull himself together. A man should know when he was lucky.

"Aren't you hungry by now?" he asked.

"Ravenous."

"Then let's go downstairs and get something to eat." He rose, putting out a hand for her, and led her toward a small curtained archway. Behind it was a flight of stairs that seemed to go down forever, until at last they found themselves in a dimly lit room.

There was a small stage, with a space left clear in
front, and around that were tables. A step up from
them were more tables, but these were enclosed in
semi-private booths.

This wasn't a restaurant, Helena realized, but a
nightclub. She'd never been in one before, and she
looked around her, taking it all in.

An important-looking man in evening dress approached, and Bruce spoke to him in a lowered voice,
although just loud enough for Helena to hear. "Look,
Joe, I don't have a reservation—"

"For you there is always a table," the man assured
him. He made an imperious gesture to an underling.
"Number seven."

Bruce took Helena's hand again and led her toward
a booth in the far corner. The booths were completely
enclosed on three sides, giving a fair amount of privacy, and instead of individual chairs there was a
semicircular bench attached to the inside wall of the
booth.

A waiter hovered respectfully over them, ignoring
diners who had been waiting longer. He obviously
knew Bruce and could anticipate his wants. Helena let
him choose everything. She was absorbed in watching
him. She had a vague memory that they had been going to talk about her problems, but he hadn't mentioned them and she was disinclined to raise the
subject now. It was easier simply to float on the magical tide that was carrying her on an adventure.

Dinner was served and she tried caviar for the first
time in her life. She found the taste too salty and
hastily washed it away with some wine. It was followed by a meal she'd never even heard of, cooked in
wine and herbs and flambéed at the table.

Somehow the conversation seemed to rise effortlessly onto an intellectual level. Bruce was talking about philosophy, but doing so lightly and in a way that made her laugh. Concepts and rationalizations floated into her brain, easily finding a niche so that she had the heady sense of holding the key to the most difficult questions. She wasn't sure whether her comprehension had grown or whether Bruce simply had the gift of making everything clear, but she was excited by the feeling of dancing among the stars.

The extent of his mind exhilarated her. Through the doors he was opening she could glimpse great vistas and long corridors leading to mysteries. He was taking her by the hand, inviting her to explore great possibilities, and she was hurrying to follow where he led.

He fell silent at last and sat smiling at her. Around them the lights were dimming, except for the little stage, where a singer had appeared.

She wore a slinky dress, and she sang in a soft throaty voice. Her songs were sensual invitations to erotic paradise, every note resonant of physical delight. Sometimes the mood changed and became an aching lament for past love, but the sultry tones left no doubt that it was the loss of passion that was being mourned.

In the dim light Helena could see Bruce's face, the dark eyes watching her closely. She felt as if he were hypnotizing her. He reached out a hand and brushed her cheek, and a tremor went right through her body. Still holding her eyes with his own, he stretched out his other hand so that the fingers met behind her head. She felt him fumbling with pins, and the next moment her hair tumbled about her shoulders.

Bruce smiled. "That's better," he said.

He still had one arm around her shoulders, and he drew her gently against him. The next moment his lips brushed lightly against hers. It was the merest whisper, but she gasped at the sensation. Her pulses were racing madly.

"Why don't we dance?" he murmured.

She didn't want to move out of the privacy of the booth, but when they were on the dance floor she realized that they were still private. No one had any attention to spare for them. The little floor was packed with couples holding each other tightly, lost in their own dreamworld.

As soon as Bruce drew her close, Helena knew that she'd been deluding herself with thoughts about his mind. It was his body she wanted; the hard, lean, vibrant and intensely male body that seemed to promise so much. He was holding her so near that she could feel the movement of his thighs against her own, and the sensation sent hot visions through her brain. There was power in every line of him, but subtlety, too, both carrying the promise of ecstasy.

Bruce felt as if he'd died and gone to paradise. In the unlikely event of his actually getting there he was sure it would be exactly like this; dancing with this gloriously beautiful woman, feeling her soft body next to his. Her erotic perfume filled his nostrils, sending his senses into a dizzy spiral of delight. The tight, figure-hugging dress left nothing to his imagination. The feel of her delicate curves was an inspiration, and her liquid movements nearly drove him wild.

He spoke her name, and when she looked up he laid his lips on hers. "Bruce," she protested faintly. "Not here—"

"Why not here?" he murmured. "Why not everywhere?"

What little clear thought he had left warned him that she was right. It was a mistake to kiss her in public because he couldn't kiss her without wanting more—wanting everything. But he couldn't *not* kiss her...again...and then again...

"Helena—" he whispered.

Her mouth framed the word yes, and he was about to ask her to leave with him, but checked himself. It was too soon—not for him, but for her. He couldn't risk losing her by rushing things.

"We'd better sit down," he said reluctantly. "You're dangerous for me."

"Dangerous? How?" she said recklessly.

"In all sorts of ways, temptress."

She laughed delightedly. She'd turned into someone else, sloughing off the skin of the sedate Miss Walker, becoming an exotic creature luring her chosen man onward to where the road vanished into a distant, thrilling horizon. She laughed again, shaking her mane about her shoulders, and several men turned to look at her with hot eyes. "Come along," Bruce said firmly, slipping his arm around her waist and drawing her away from them.

At the table he spoke a word in the ear of the waiter, and a moment later a single red rose appeared, which Bruce kissed and handed to her. In her new self she knew instinctively how to respond to such gallantry, kissing the rose exactly where he had kissed it, then breaking off the head and tucking it into the front of her dress. Bruce looked at it nestling there between the soft cleft of her breasts, and had to grip the edge of his seat. It wasn't fair, he thought. It really wasn't.

The champagne that he had also ordered was delivered to the table. He poured some for her and they raised their glasses in salute. His mind was racing. To hell with not rushing things. It must be tonight. She was clearly a far more experienced woman than he'd realized before, and she wanted him as much as he wanted her.

"Helena," he said, saying her name with meaning, and taking her hand. He couldn't hear her reply through the noise, but he saw her lips shape the words "What is it?"

"Tell me what you're feeling. I want to know."

She sought for an answer, wondering how she could find words for the sweet singing sensations that pervaded her. But suddenly the air was split by a bellow of laughter. They both winced and turned their heads to see a large, red-faced man looming over them. "Hey, Brucie, old fellow," he boomed, "Fancy seeing you here!"

Bruce spoke through gritted teeth. "Hello, Angus."

Angus squeezed himself in next to Helena without waiting for an invitation. "Aren't you going to introduce me?" he demanded.

"Helena, Angus. Angus, Helena," Bruce said without enthusiasm. His face had a strained look that Helena guessed matched her own. The moment had been so exciting, but it had been snatched away from them by this vulgar buffoon.

She tried to edge away from him but he seized her hand in his and pumped it up and down. "Always glad to meet a lady friend of Bruce's," he bawled. "Blessed if I know where he finds them all. Never knew such a man for picking peaches, and they don't come much peachier than you, sweetheart."

"Are you alone tonight?" Bruce asked acidly, "or is your wife with you?"

"My wife! That's rich!" Angus went off into a storm of laughter. "Nah, I've teamed up with a little popsie for the evening. Cutest little thing you ever saw. She went off to slap some more warpaint on. There she is." He waved to a voluptuous woman who was threading her way through the crowd. "Over here, sweetie. Come and meet my friends. Folks, this is Caroline."

"Coral," the young woman corrected him edgily.

"Coral, Caroline, what's the odds as long as we're having fun?" Angus demanded. "Siddown over there with Bruce, sweetie, while I get to know this little—"

"I'm afraid we have to go," Bruce declared firmly, rising and drawing Helena to her feet. "It's a pleasure to meet you Coral, but we were just leaving."

"Aw, c'mon," Angus urged, breathing alcohol fumes over everyone. "The night is young. We've each got a pretty little friend and I thought we might do a swa—"

"*Goodnight,*" Bruce said in a voice of such freezing danger that the smile faded from Angus's face. He didn't say another word as they left the nightclub, and Helena was glad of that because she needed time to come to terms with what had happened. Angus's vulgar intrusion had shattered the spell in which she'd been held, showing her the whole scene in a new, trashy light.

He'd thought she was a popsie because she looked like a popsie. Maybe she'd even been acting like one: horrid thought. She gave a little shiver.

"Hey, what is it?" Bruce asked, slipping an arm around her shoulder. "Don't let Angus worry you. He's just a clown who doesn't matter."

"I suppose so," she said, trying to cheer up. She felt suddenly cold. "I think I should go home now."

Bruce was about to say "The night is young," as he'd said many times before, but somehow he couldn't get the words out. The mood was gone. He put his arm around her shoulders and they strolled toward the car. When they were inside Helena saw the clock on the dashboard, and started. "That can't really be the time?"

"Who cares about time?"

"Your 'Alastair-sitter' will, for one."

"Forget him. He's swotting for his college entrance and works half the night away. Let's take a drive to the edge of beyond."

"It sounds lovely, but I have to go home," she said reluctantly.

He sighed. "So do I. All right. Let's go."

When he finally drew up outside her home he switched off the engine and turned to her. "I'm really sorry it ended like that," he said quietly. "I hated for you to be upset."

"It doesn't matter. It was that kind of place."

"Perhaps I shouldn't have taken you to that kind of place. It was just that—" He drew in his breath slowly at the wonder of her loveliness. "You're so... beautiful," he whispered, taking her face between his hands.

The moment their lips touched, the spell began again. He kissed her with tender urgency, caressing her mouth with restraint, which gradually faded as his passion rose. He dropped his hands from her face and took her wholly into his arms. Her head seemed to find its natural position against his shoulder, and her own passion flared up in response to his. No man's embrace had ever made her feel like this, as though she were drowning in sensual pleasure. Every part of her body was pervaded by physical delight, such as she'd never known before, never even believed possible. Her nature was cautious, but this joyful new sensation made a mockery of caution. Here in his arms it was easy to believe that nothing else mattered as long as she could stay here forever.

His tongue eased its way into her mouth and began a slow exploration that sent her wild with pleasure. There was subtlety and experience in his kiss. He knew how to restrain his own desire while evoking hers, and she relaxed, giving herself up totally to the glorious experience. Each time the tip of his tongue glided softly across the tender inner surface of her mouth, a tremor went through her until it reached the fire that was growing deep in her loins.

He stroked her face with his free hand, letting the fingertips trail softly downward to her neck. With every touch a new ember was added to the flames that flared higher every moment, threatening to consume her. How could a woman be possessed by such heat? she wondered wildly. It seemed at any moment she must explode.

He began to cover her face with small kisses, her mouth, her nose, her eyelids, then the tender place beneath her ears. She moaned softly, trying to keep up with the myriad sensations that chased themselves through her trembling flesh. When his lips began to drift down her neck to the base of her throat, she clung to him, ready to yield totally. The deep plunging neckline meant that her breasts were almost exposed to his caresses, ready for him, aching with eagerness....

Through her half-opened eyes she could see the house over his shoulder. Her gaze fixed on the front room beside the door, which she knew was Sally's bedroom. The realization seemed to freeze her. "Bruce..." she murmured reluctantly. "Not here..."

He raised his head and spoke unsteadily. "Let me come inside with you."

"No—please—I never meant this to happen."

An urgent note in her voice got through to him and he forced himself to release her. Helena drew quickly back from him, trying to regain control of herself. "I'd better go inside," she said unsteadily.

She escaped and headed up the steps to the front door. Bruce followed her. "Are you angry with me?" he asked anxiously.

"No—it's me. I just—I'm confused, that's all. Please . . . I have to go."

"Can't I come in for a minute?" he pleaded.

She was on the verge of saying yes to anything he wanted, but some last vestige of caution was still alive and waving. "Better not," she said with a sigh. "I must go and try to get some sleep. I have classes to take tomorrow, books to mark..."

He groaned. "Tell me about it. Classes, conferences, all the dreary paraphernalia of routine. How I'm going to endure it I can't—well anyway, to hell with all that. I want to take you on a picnic and drink wine with you in the sun."

"Mmm, lovely," she said wistfully.

"We'll do it this weekend. Say yes."

"Yes."

"Then I suppose I can let you go. Goodnight." He kissed her again. It was the briefest touch this time, but the instant flare-up between them was a warning.

"You must go home," Helena said unwillingly.

He sighed. "Yes, I suppose I must." He kissed the tip of her nose. "That's as much as I dare allow myself. Goodnight, loveliest Helena."

She watched him return to the car, and stood on the step until his rear lights had vanished, then went in as quietly as she could. She seemed to float on air as she climbed the stairs.

Once in her tiny flat she didn't turn on the light, but sat in the darkness, trying to come to terms with the shattering thing that had happened to her. Until now, her romances had been quiet affairs, made up of fondness and gentle kisses. None of them had induced in her this violence of erotic feeling, this wild sensuality that colored all the world. But Bruce had changed everything. In his arms she'd discovered the truth about her own explosive sexuality, and now there was no going back. The new woman she'd become was vitally aware of her own body and its possibilities. She was aware of his body, too, and what she wanted from it. It had been the hardest decision of her life to send him away tonight.

But perhaps there would be other nights, she thought with a little smile, nights when she wouldn't send him away, and they would be free to discover passion together.

She put on the lamp and rose to her feet. As she did so, something on the sofa fell to the floor. Picking it up, she discovered that it was the book Sally had been reading. Helena glanced at the title, *Heavenly Conjunctions,* remembering that Sally had said Bruce was reading this early that morning. He'd spilled his coffee on it. She flicked through until she found the page with the faint, damp stain. Smiling, she began to read.

As she read, her smile faded and an ominous look took its place.

Vibrant, passionate Miss Leo, is the mate created by Heaven for roving-eyed Mr. Sagittarius, declared the book. *She doesn't feel threatened by his need for freedom, because she knows that her tempestuous sexuality will keep him coming home. She won't nag or demand explanations because she knows he can't be tied down. In fact, for Sagittarius man, Miss Leo can be the perfect, undemanding playmate.*

"Can she?" Helena breathed, eyes glittering. "Can she, indeed?"

Chapter Six

Bruce came out of his happy dream long enough to say, "What have I always told you about reading at the table?"

Alastair raised his head from the book. "You've said that it's impolite," he recited obediently.

"Then why are you doing it?"

"Because you do it, too."

"So I do." Bruce yawned. "But you should have finished your homework last night."

"I *did* finish it last night," Alastair protested with an air of injured innocence. "I had plenty of time to finish it because you were so late. I got really worried about you—"

"Cut it out," Bruce said, grinning. "If that book isn't homework, what is it? Astrology. I might have known."

"It's fascinating to see which other people have certain signs. You, for instance, share your sign with Jane Fonda, Frank Sinatra and Beethoven."

"Do I indeed? And who does Miss W—Miss Leo share her sign with?"

If Alastair noticed his hasty correction he showed no sign of it, but riffled through pages. "Napoleon, Mussolini and Alfred Hitchcock," he said innocently.

"You'll go too far one of these days."

"Lucille Ball and Jackie Onassis," Alastair added quickly.

"That's better." Bruce yawned again, and said, as if the idea had just occurred to him, "Your grandparents haven't seen you for quite a while. Why not visit them this weekend?"

"Are they expecting me?"

Bruce left the kitchen and dialed a number on the hall phone. After talking for a few minutes he returned, saying, "Grandpa says he's found a new fishing spot that you'll love. I'll drive you over there tonight."

"That's lovely." Alastair spoke with real enthusiasm, but his eyes were puzzled.

"Now I suppose we'd better get going to school," Bruce said.

He was too preoccupied with his own blissful thoughts to notice his nephew's air of suppressed excitement. Alastair stayed suspiciously quiet as they drove to school, but once there he rushed off to find Sally and compare notes about the previous night.

"Half past three in the morning," Alastair told her with satisfaction. "My 'companion' had got fed up waiting and gone to sleep on the sofa. He wasn't pleased. Apparently Uncle Bruce had said he expected to be home much earlier."

"They said goodbye on the front step at three o'clock. I heard them just by my bedroom window." Sally sighed romantically. "They sounded ever so stuck on each other. They're going on a picnic this weekend."

"So that's why I've suddenly been packed off to my grandparents for the weekend," Alastair said. "Then it's even more important to do an in-depth study of their suitability. What about the year Miss Walker was born? Any luck?"

"I tried to work around to it subtly last night, talking about people getting older quicker in history. Only she saw through it and said she wasn't going to tell me how old she was. But luckily she gave me a lift this morning, and stopped at a gas station. She left her drivers' license in the car, so I took a quick look at it."

"Good work! What's the year?"

She told him and he scribbled it down. "You're quite sure you noted it correctly?" he asked.

"Of course I'm sure," said his affronted henchwoman.

"Just checking. You can't be too careful with so much at stake." Then, because he came under Aquarius, a sign noted for its social adroitness, he added, "Tell me your date and I'll do a chart for you, as well."

The bell had just gone for the start of the morning break when a pupil approached Helena with a message. "Mr. Venables says, could he see you in his office please, Miss Walker?"

"Thank you." Helena gathered up her books and walked briskly to the Headmaster's Office. A night of furious thought had left her pale but determined. If Bruce Venables thought she was going to be an understanding little playmate, in the Coral mold, he had another think coming.

The problem was, how to make him understand that things were at an end between them, without actually admitting how she'd reached her conclusion. "I saw your coffee stain in a book on astrology" wasn't exactly dignified.

Mrs. Conrad, Bruce's secretary, smiled and nodded her in, but Bruce himself opened the door and spoke in a magisterial tone. "Ah, Miss Walker, I hope you've brought those schedules for me to look over."

"Certainly, Mr. Venables," she responded severely, and went before him into the office.

As soon as the door was closed, Bruce reached for her, but she slid gracefully out of his way. "It's all right," he protested. "We're alone now. I had to put on that little act for the benefit of my secretary, but she can't see through an oak door. Wait." He put his head back around the door to say, "You can go to lunch now, Mrs. Conrad."

When he'd closed the door again he made another attempt to put his arms around her, but again Helena evaded him. "Darling..." he protested.

"I think it would be more proper for you to call me Miss Walker," Helena informed him coolly.

"I do—when there are other people around. But when we're alone I'm going to call you my lovely Helena."

He said the last words in a soft voice that sent shivers of pleasure through her body. It was her first experience of desire that had a will of its own, that was so uncontrollable that it could defy her mind's decisions. But she fought back and clung to her resolve, looking him in the eye to say steadily, "Since we're not going to be alone there'll be no occasion for hyperbole."

He winced. "Must you talk to me as though you were marking the essay of a recalcitrant pupil?"

"Mr. Venables, did you send for me to discuss school matters, because if not I have things to see to."

"Hang them! You know why I sent for you. Why are you suddenly acting like a frozen prune?"

"I'm acting the way I should have acted from the start. You're the headmaster of this school and I'm one of your staff. We should never have allowed ourselves to forget that for a moment. It was unprofessional."

Bruce ran a hand distractedly through his hair. "All right, I'll grant that trying to kiss you in my study wasn't strictly in accordance with the book of staff etiquette, but I couldn't help myself. I can't stop thinking about kissing you. It may be unprofessional but it's true." He smiled at her. "What are we going to do about it?"

"I don't know what *you're* going to do," she declared, trying to calm her racing pulse, "but I'm returning to my classroom."

He stopped her with a hand on her arm. "What about our picnic?"

"Haven't you been listening to a word I've said? No kissing, no picnic, no personal relationship. Nothing. Do I make myself quite clear?"

Bruce's expression hardened. "Perfectly. The only thing I don't understand is what's happened to you since last night. When we said good-night on your step, you were very different. And when I kissed you—''

"That's enough," she said firmly. "That kiss should never have happened. As far as I'm concerned it *didn't* happen—''

"The hell it didn't! It happened all right. I kissed you and you kissed me. That is a fact. To be precise, it's two facts, both of them highly enjoyable. There were other enjoyable things about the evening, like the way you were dressed—''

She stiffened. "That was an accident."

"You *fell* into that dress by accident?" he demanded ironically. "Well pardon me! I was under the impression that it must have taken a shoehorn to get you in." Unwisely he voiced the thought that had been teasing and delighting him for hours. "And as for getting you out of it—''

Helena's eyes flashed. "Now we come to the point, don't we?"

Bruce blinked. "Pardon?"

"The whole point of the evening. I should have woken up a lot sooner than I did. It was only after I got home that I—that something made me realize the shabby game you were really playing."

"You've lost me."

"I am not going to be your little playmate, Bruce, and you should have known better than to think I would."

If he'd had the sense to declare that he didn't see her in that light, which was half true, all might have been made well there and then. But a strong sense of being ill-used made him take the brakes off his tongue, not for the first time, and turn disaster into calamity. "Oh really?'' he seethed. ''Well let me tell you, that was one helluva 'playmate' dress you were wearing.''

''I didn't *mean* to wear it.''

''That conjures up some interesting pictures. I suppose a bandit hopped in through your window, waved a gun at you and forced you to put on that extremely sexy dress, not to mention that even sexier perfume.''

Helena gave a little gasp of horror. ''Oh no! Don't tell me you could smell that?''

''Don't tell me—? *What? That's* the best line I've ever heard—or the most cynical, I'm not sure. I suppose that was another accident.''

''Sally sprayed it over me before I could stop her. It belongs to my landlady.''

''Come on. You can do better than that. I caught a glimpse of your landlady when I arrived last night, and a more unlikely candidate for *L'Eternité d'Amour* I can't imagine.''

''I see you recognized it,'' Helena responded through gritted teeth. ''No doubt you know it very well.''

''I . . . am acquainted with it,'' Bruce replied cautiously, seeing quagmires approaching.

''I'll bet you're more than acquainted with it. I'll bet it's standard among your playmates.''

''Only the more discerning of them. What has that got to do with us?''

''Think about it,'' she flashed.

''I'm trying. The only thing that occurs to me is that if you expect me to believe it came from Mrs. Carter, you've taken leave of your senses. Look, I thought we were going to have a sedate, friendly evening. I promised you that and I'd have stuck by my word. But you came on strong.''

"I never—"

"Oh, yes you did, *Miss* Walker. Don't blame me for being human. I'm only speaking aloud the things I was thinking last night—things, I might add, that your get-up was designed to make me think. Don't misunderstand me. I'm not criticizing. I'm admiring. At least, I admired you then. I'm just sorry that this morning you don't have the courage of last night's convictions. Or is it worse than a case of cold feet? Was the whole performance nothing but the work of a calculating, cold-hearted tease?"

For answer Helena whirled and pushed the window wide open. "Why don't you shout a little louder?" she inquired with glacial irony. "There might be a few people on the far side of town who don't know all the details of our private business yet."

Then she walked out, leaving Bruce with his head in his hands.

Sally accompanied her mother to the hospital that evening, so Helena had the flat to herself, to brood.

She was furiously angry, with herself as much as with Bruce. He was devious, unscrupulous and calculating, but she'd known that from the very first moment when he'd used George's illness to steal his job. She'd allowed superficial attraction to blind her to those facts, and last night she'd had a sharp reminder.

When she thought of how he'd deliberately aroused her dormant sexuality for his own cynical ends she wanted to explode. It was the merest chance that he'd left a clue to reveal what he was up to. She'd been lucky in discovering everything *before any damage was done.* She repeated the last words to herself very firmly.

But it took too much energy to keep anger at fever pitch for long. At last it ran down and she was left facing the fact that it hurt. He'd enticed her into a beautiful dream and the awakening was painful. Besides which, only her mind had seen the truth. Her body was still back in the dream. It had flowered under Bruce's touch and it craved for him still. It shocked her that she could still want a man whom she knew to be a bad character, but it was too late. The spell had been cast, and it would take time and hard work to break it. But break it she would.

On Sunday evening Alastair's grandfather drove him home but, being in a hurry, dropped him on the step, checked through the intercom that Bruce was at home, and departed. Alastair stepped out of the lift a few moments later to find Bruce standing by the open front door. The boy was bright-eyed and brown-skinned after a happy weekend's fishing.

Uncle and nephew hugged each other. "Supper's ready," Bruce announced.

"Oh, good. I'm starving."

"Meaning you haven't eaten for a whole hour, I suppose," Bruce said wryly. "Have a good time?"

Alastair proceeded to give him a detailed account between mouthfuls, which Bruce, whose interest in fishing was nil, bore with fortitude. At last even Alastair's enthusiasm was satisfied, and he asked, "What about you, Uncle Bruce? Did you have a good time?"

"Me? Oh yes, great, fantastic." He had, in fact, spent the weekend trying to complete an article for a literary periodical and discovering that his customary facility had deserted him. A young woman with a tawny mane and flashing eyes kept distracting him. He'd tried to banish her, but he couldn't forget that instead of sitting in front of a word processor he should have been on a picnic with her, reclining in the grass and watching the sunlight turn her hair to gold. "Fantastic," he repeated, adding with a grin, "Without you around, the place was wonderfully peaceful."

"No, I mean the picnic," Alastair persisted. "Did you enjoy that?"

Bruce stared at him. "Picnic? I never told you I was going on a picnic."

Various expressions passed across Alastair's face, all of them indicative of a boy genius whose mighty intellect had been betrayed by a moment's forgetfulness, and who now found himself in the soup. "Didn't you?" he asked innocently. "Are you sure?"

"Quite sure," Bruce replied implacably. "What put the idea of a picnic into your head? And don't try being clever with me."

"In that case, I knew you were going on a picnic with Miss Walker."

"How?"

"Uncle," Alastair said in shocked accents, "you wouldn't want me to betray a confidence, would you?"

Bruce eyed him in exasperation. "I suppose Sally comes into this somewhere?"

"My lips are sealed," Alastair said with dignity.

Bruce took a deep, slow breath and counted to ten. Inwardly he was reliving the goodnight on Helena's doorstep. That was when he'd suggested the picnic.

And Sally. Where had she been? Somewhere just inside the house, hanging on every word. He groaned, wishing he could sink through the floor. "All right," he said, speaking with difficulty. "You didn't betray your partner in crime. I guessed. So now, for heaven's sake, stop being a martyr to your conscience and speak plainly. I suppose it's all around the school by now?"

Alastair drew himself up in righteous indignation. "Certainly not, Uncle. This is private."

"That's what I thought, but it seems I was wrong."

"Sally and I take an interest merely in a spirit of scientific inquiry."

"You've lost me."

"Astrologically speaking, you and Miss Walker are perfectly matched," Alastair explained in the manner of a professor lecturing an attentive but slow-witted student. "The interest lay in seeing whether the practice matched the theory."

Bruce eyed him in fascination, realizing that he'd never plumbed Alastair's depths before. He'd been thinking of himself as a man enthralled by a woman, and it turned out that he'd actually been a specimen under the microscope of a midget demon scientist. "And what conclusions did you come to?" he asked faintly.

"Now you're asking me to theorize ahead of my data."

"Pardon?"

"I can't draw conclusions until I know how the picnic went."

"There was no picnic," Bruce said through gritted teeth. "I got stood up. So you can go back to your scientific colleague and tell her that the practice doesn't match the theory at all. Maybe the two of you can present a paper on it to the Royal Society. It should be worth a fellowship at least."

But irony was wasted on Alastair. "Stood up?" he echoed, with furrowed brow. "You mean, Miss Walker changed her mind?"

"Yes."

"Without good reason?"

"Yes," Bruce repeated, wondering if this conversation proved he was mad.

"Most mysterious, especially after Sally took such trouble to ensure success."

"After she *what?*"

"I must admit I was a little troubled when she told me what she'd done in case it interfered with the purity of the experiment, but when she explained how Miss Walker had undone all her work, I concluded that—"

"Alastair, I will give you three seconds to tell me exactly what Sally did."

"Nothing much. She just used some of her mother's perfume."

"Her mother—you mean, Mrs. Carter—*her* perfume?" Bruce asked, choosing his words with care.

"That's right. Her brother gave it to her, only she never uses it. So Sally sprayed it all over Miss Walker. She thought she'd be pleased, but she wasn't. She scrubbed it all off and insisted on changing her clothes. So it couldn't really have made any difference at all, could it?"

"Not a bit," Bruce assured him, relieved to discover there were still some gaps in his precocious nephew's knowledge. "You, er, don't happen to know what she was wearing before she changed?"

"The same clothes she was wearing at school that day," Alastair said serenely. "Can I have some more milk?"

"Here. Then you'd better get to bed. And may I suggest that you kill the experiment? It was always a non-starter."

"But, Uncle—"

"I'll put it another way. Butt out if you know what's good for you."

"Yes, Uncle."

When Alastair had gone to bed Bruce was free to sort out his shattered thoughts. Chief among them was an appalled vision of the neat blouse and skirt Helena had worn at school. That was how she'd meant to present herself. She hadn't even known she was still wearing the perfume. The "seductive temptress" had been, as she'd claimed, an accident.

But why did she change into that particular dress? his other self pleaded.

He dismissed the thought. That was nit-picking. The truth was that he'd gotten it all wrong and offended her again. She really was as he'd first thought of her, sweet and natural and unselfconsciously lovely. They could have started a beautiful relationship if he'd stuck to his word and encouraged her to talk about her lift trauma. Instead they hadn't even touched on it once.

He groaned. "You fool," he told himself. "She was special as she was, and you knew that. You should have trusted your first instincts. You had it all in your hands, and you blew it, *you blew it,* YOU BLEW IT."

As spring turned into summer, the days became warm and sunny, and Helena was sometimes tempted to hold a class outside, with her pupils sitting on the grass beneath the huge old oak tree that graced the grounds. The fresh air seemed to make them more alert, and some lively discussions ensued. If her pupils had strong opinions she took this as an encouraging sign and seldom intervened in disputes except to keep the noise down.

"Who else thinks Queen Elizabeth the first has been overrated?" she asked one morning to quell an incipient riot between the pros and the antis. A fair number of hands went up. "All right, Peter, let's hear what you think."

"She could never make her mind up," said a tousle-haired boy at the back. "Because she was a queen, everyone said it was subtle diplomacy, but actually she was just dithering." With twelve-year-old chauvinism, he added, "Just like a woman."

Helena joined in the general laugh, but suddenly realized it contained an unfamiliar element. Turning, she saw Bruce standing, almost concealed by the tree. "Good morning, Mr. Venables," she said politely.

"Good morning, Miss Walker. Don't let me interrupt the lesson. I was enjoying it." He seated himself on the ground beside the pupils and turned his face up to her attentively.

Helena took a breath to calm herself, resolving to continue exactly as before. She wasn't ashamed of her style of teaching and she wasn't going to let Bruce Venables think she was worried about his opinion. But the words "simplistic to the point of falsity" flitted through her head.

"Surely the girls aren't going to let Peter get away with that?" she inquired, looking away from him and out over the sea of faces. "You, Delia?"

"I think most of what people call subtle diplomacy these days is just dithering," Delia asserted defiantly.

"Very good point. Anyone else?"

"Personally I'm scared to death by Queen Elizabeth," Bruce said irrepressibly. "Always have been."

He cocked an inquiring eyebrow at the belligerent Delia, encouraging her to come back with, "Men just don't like a woman in power who can do without men."

"She didn't," Peter yelled at her indignantly. "It was men who did everything. They fought all the battles, and attacked foreign ships and—and everything. She just sat on her throne dithering."

A dozen voices rose in agreement or complaint, but they were drowned by the sound of the bell. "All right, off for your break," Helena called, and a stampede began back to school. To Helena's satisfaction, Delia and Peter appeared to be continuing the argument as they ran. She gathered her books.

"Well done," Bruce said, picking one up and handing it to her. "I haven't often seen youngsters really involved like that. You've got the gift of making it live for them."

Helena derived a moment of grim pleasure from this praise by the man who'd been so critical of her abilities, but she didn't let it show. To her annoyance her heart had begun beating madly at his nearness. "Thank you," she said coolly.

"Does it come naturally, or did you learn it from someone?"

"A little of both," she said, facing him. "I've always preferred to teach by getting my pupils involved, but George helped me refine the method. He was a great encouragement."

"George?"

"George Fletcher," she said with biting emphasis. "The headmaster of this school. Remember him?"

A look of unmistakable embarrassment passed across Bruce's face. "Ah, yes," he said hastily. "That George."

"Yes, *that* George. You didn't even know who I meant, did you? That's disgraceful."

"Helena—"

"You might have had the grace to remember his name, since you're only supposed to be holding the fort for him."

There was an uneasy silence, and Helena realized that she'd taken him by surprise. "What...exactly do you mean by that?" he asked cautiously.

"Well, you're only the *acting* head, aren't you? And acting means temporary, doesn't it?"

"Look...I don't want to go into this just now—"

"I'll bet you don't. It would really have surprised me if you felt able to discuss how you came to be in this job."

Bruce's face hardened with anger. She'd never seen it like that before. "How I came to be in this job is my own affair," he said coldly. "I'm not going to be held accountable by you and that's final."

"Then there's nothing more to be said," she snapped. "Now, if you'll let me pass, I have things to do."

For answer he took firm hold of her elbow and sat down on the bench that ran around the tree. Helena was forced to sit down beside him or engage in an undignified struggle under the gaze of pupils who were walking through the grounds. "Let me go at once," she seethed. "How dare you behave like this!"

"You don't give me any choice. You won't come to my office when I ask you to, and I can hardly waylay you in the corridor. Just keep calm and anyone who sees us will think we're discussing school business."

"We have *nothing* to discuss."

"Oh, that's great!" he exclaimed furiously. "You've had your say, but the minute I want mine, the conversation is over. As young Peter would say, just like a woman." With disconcerting suddenness the anger died out of his face. "Helena, please let's not quarrel. I'm trying to apologize."

"Very well. You've apologized. Goodbye." She tried to rise but Bruce's hand never moved and she was forced to give in. "I'll never forgive you for this," she said bitterly.

"Well, that makes two things you'll never forgive me for. I don't seem to have much to lose. I don't know when I'll manage to catch up with you again, so I'd better make the most of it. It's about that night— I know a good deal now that I didn't know then, and it explains a lot. I've discovered, for instance, that when you said Sally sprayed you with perfume you were telling the truth."

"Well, that's nice to know," she retorted with frosty irony. "How delightful that my honesty has been cleared on the word of a child."

He tore his hair with his free hand. "All right, I put it tactlessly. I'm sorry. It's a habit of mine. Things just come out sounding wrong. I try to change it but I can't."

"Oh, don't change it. At least it tells me what you're really thinking. Now I know that you thought I was a liar."

"Well, you have to admit that the story sounded a bit unlikely. But now I know it's true. I even know why it happened."

He waited, hoping her curiosity would get the better of her. But it didn't and he was forced to give in. "I also know that you were going to wear that very prissy blouse and skirt you'd been wearing during the day. So you didn't mean to appear—" He hesitated because the memory of how she'd looked that night was making his head swim. "To appear...exactly how you appeared, and I'm sorry I misunderstood everything."

Helena regarded him suspiciously but there was a hint of softening in her eyes. He might have made it home, had not an incurable passion for academic truth caused him to add, "Of course, there's still the question of why you chose that particular dress—"

"A question that you'll doubtless answer for your own convenience," she said frostily. "Once and for all, before I tried that dress on I had no idea what it looked like—"

"Come on!" he cried skeptically, good resolutions forgotten. "Making every allowance—"

"Don't make allowance for me, Mr. Venables, because I'm not making any for you. The other night was a mistake and I learn from my mistakes. I do *not* repeat them. From now on we go our own ways and give each other a wide berth. Now I'm going to get up, and if you don't release me at once I shall ignore professional etiquette and do something extremely painful to your shins."

She pulled her arm free and walked away from him across the grass, leaving Bruce to the despairing reflection that he'd blown it again.

Chapter Seven

It was satisfactory, Helena felt, to have the matter of Bruce Venables over and done with. As the days became a week, and then two weeks, it was clear that he'd accepted his dismissal. She was glad he'd decided to be sensible. Very glad, indeed. She told herself that often.

It was true that sometimes she would lie awake in the early hours, her body aching with unaccustomed frustration. She had experienced the reality of passion in one blazing, beautiful night, but it had been cruelly snatched away before she could find fulfillment. The man who'd made her body sing for the first time was a carelessly cynical lover. He was not for her, or for any woman who wanted to take love seriously.

She applied academic logic to the problem. It was ridiculous and unreasonable to pine for something she'd discovered so recently. But some discoveries cannot be reversed, and the memory of his lips on her lips, on her neck, on her breasts, could not be banished. It rose in the darkness to torment her with longing for what she had given up. By day she never went where she might encounter him. It was bad enough to have to attend school assembly and listen to the deep, vibrant music of his voice.

Worse still were the moments when her flesh was quiet but her heart ached for the light that had been in his eyes when he smiled, or a note of gentleness that could come into his voice. In the past her head had always ruled her heart without effort. But now her heart grew rebellious and longed for forbidden fruit.

She strove not to think of him. It would soon be time for Parents' Evening when the families of the pupils could visit the school, and ask the staff about their children. Helena plunged into preparatory work, spending long evenings going over the records of all her pupils so that she would be ready to answer any questions.

On the actual day of the event, classes finished early. Immediately work began on turning the building into a reception center. Refreshment tables were set up, displays of schoolwork were arranged around the walls, and several of the older, more reliable pupils were deputed to act as hosts and hostesses. When the doors were opened, a large crowd of parents had already built up.

Helena had tried to snatch a coffee and sausage roll before she started but there wasn't time. She chatted cheerfully to parents until she was weary. To her dismay there was still a queue waiting to talk to her. She rubbed her eyes, then removed her hand and wondered if she was dreaming. A cup of coffee had appeared magically on the desk before her. "Drink up," came Bruce's voice above her head. "You look as if you need it."

She looked up quickly, but he had already turned away, shaking hands with visitors and smiling, so that she might have imagined it but for the hot, delicious coffee with the merest trace of sugar, just as she liked it.

A disgruntled male voice said, "He's certainly made himself at home here."

Andrew Jenks seated himself in front of her. He was a large, middle-aged man with a semi-permanent scowl. He was also a member of the local council, had a son at Edenbrook, and was one of the school governors. Helena had met him before and knew him to be prickly but basically kind. "You sound as if you don't like Mr. Venables?" she said.

"I didn't like the way he was forced on us," the councillor growled.

Helena stared. "*Forced* on you? But I thought the governors were falling over themselves to beg him to take the job."

"Some of them were. Not me. I thought the deputy head would have been ideal, and said so. But there were voices that could shout louder than mine, and did." He leaned over the table in conspiratorial fashion. "I can tell you, there had been some very determined lobbying going on."

"Lobbying—by whom?" Helena asked, bewildered.

"Let's say the smooth-talking Bruce Venables was determined to have this job and he arranged to be asked. He knew everyone that mattered."

"Yes," Helena seethed. "I'll bet he did."

"Er, you don't mind my talking about him like this, do you? He's not a friend of yours, or anything?"

"Not even 'or anything,'" she said firmly.

"Good. Hey, aren't you going to finish your coffee?"

"I don't think so. It might choke me."

At last the numbers began to thin out. For twenty minutes, nobody visited Helena's table. She yawned and started gathering up her things, but out of the corner of her eye she saw a man seat himself in front of her. "I'd like to discuss my nephew," he said.

She looked wryly at Bruce. "I doubt I can tell you anything about Alastair that you don't already know. And I'd like to go home."

"But my nephew is one of your pupils and I want to ask you about his progress. Are you refusing?"

"Certainly not," she said, getting her wits together. "Alastair's progress has been excellent in all subjects. In fact, he's so far ahead that I think the time has come to do what you once mentioned, and move him up a form."

His eyes gleamed. "Is that a clever way of getting rid of me, Helena?"

"Certainly not, *Mr. Venables*. I'd never make such a suggestion unless I was sure it was for Alastair's good."

"No, of course you wouldn't. I apologize. The thing is, I'm now in two minds about moving him on. Perhaps you can advise me."

"As far as his work's concerned, he's more than ready for it."

"True, but there's more in life than work, isn't there?"

"I don't know what you mean."

"There's friendship, for a start. The academic benefit of moving him up should be weighed against the problems he might have in making friends so far out of his own age group. He manages pretty well with children two years older than himself, but three years might be too much. He's as thick as thieves with Sally. Perhaps he should stay in her form. What do you think?"

"I've always felt there was more to be considered than just letting him race ahead academically," she reminded him.

"And I'm partly conceding your point." Bruce's manner was impeccably judicious. The past might not have existed. "The difficulty comes in deciding whether he really gains from Sally's troublemaker influence or not."

"Troublemaker?" Helena echoed, startled. "Sally?"

"Well, maybe it's his mischievous influence over her. Or perhaps it's a case of folie à deux—two people egging each other on to acts of madness that neither would have performed individually."

"Thank you, I do know what folie à deux means," Helena said crisply, "but I'm at a loss to know how it applies here. Just what 'acts of madness' do you have in mind?"

"Well, perhaps acts of mischief might be a better description." He eyed her curiously. "Do you mean, you don't know anything about it?"

"Not a thing," she said, beginning to feel nervous.

"Then I'd better show you." Bruce delved into his briefcase and produced several large sheets of paper that he laid on the table between them.

"What on earth are these?" she inquired, trying to take in the complex charts that were spread out before her.

"The documents in the case, Miss Walker. Documents that will repay your earnest study. Haven't you ever seen astrological charts before?"

"But whose—?"

"Yours and mine. Alastair must have spent hours over these. Even I can see that he's done them very well, with commendable attention to detail."

"The sun in Saturn," she murmured, sounding dazed. "The moon in Jupiter... Mercury rising in the seventh house... ascendant sign..."

"Yes, they're beautifully precise, aren't they? You need the exact moment of birth for this or at least to within twelve hours, so my young mentor tells me."

Helena's eyes kindled. "And just how did Alastair get my year of birth? Did you dare—?"

"Not guilty, I swear it. I imagine Sally had something to do with it."

"But what are they playing at?"

"They've decided that the stars have destined us for each other. According to Alastair, certain signs are specially compatible—or incompatible. Pisces and Scorpio go well together, while Sagittarius and Virgo are poison. But the most perfect astrological combination of them all is Leo and Sagittarius." He caught Helena's disapproving eye on him and added hastily, "So Alastair says."

"Are you researching a learned volume for the Oxford University Press on this subject?" she inquired coldly, "or do you just enjoy wasting your time and mine? If you were anything of a headmaster, never mind an uncle, you'd advise Alastair to give up this nonsense."

"*Advise Alastair?* You don't think that mad midget takes my advice, do you? I'm more likely to ask it than give it. He's got us all worked out and—"

"Just tell him he's wrong about this."

"I'm not sure that he *is* wrong. Divine predestination might account for the effect you've had on me from the first moment."

Helena surveyed him coolly. "Very clever!" she said. "I thought I knew how low you could sink, but this takes my breath away. Actually dragging a child in to do your dirty work—"

"Now wait a minute! First, I did not drag Alastair in. In fact, I told him to keep his nose out of my affairs, but he cast these anyway, and I happened to find them."

"How convenient!" she scoffed. "And what a lucky coincidence that they happened to say exactly what suited you."

"Now there, if I may say so, you've taken a lot for granted. Who says it *is* what suited me? I never wanted to fall i—become attracted to you. In fact, the whole thing was totally against my will, which would argue some divine predestination, don't you think?"

"What I think is that you're insulting my intelligence and I don't like it. How could you imagine that I'd be impressed with all this pseudo-academic talk? I can recognize high-priced tinsel wrapping when I see it."

"Why must you always think the worst of my motives?" he demanded.

"It saves time."

He sighed. "You are the most rigidly unforgiving woman I've ever known. I thought we might enjoy a laugh together over the antics of those two crazy children, but there's no bending you once you get an idea in your head, is there? To you the world is stark black or dazzling white, and people are either angels or demons with nothing in between. I don't know when or why I suddenly found myself wearing the black Stetson, but I know your simplistic view of life scares the living daylights out of me."

"That's it," she said, very pale. "It's been a long day and I'm going home."

"Helena, please—"

"I believe there's a parent over there who would like to talk to you."

Reluctantly Bruce turned and assumed a professional smile for a haughty-looking woman who was bearing down on him. Helena seized her chance to escape.

Courtesy obliged her to drive Mrs. Carter and Sally home, although she would have been glad to escape Sally's company for a while. It was a relief when Mrs. Carter said, "I'll be taking Sally to the hospital tomorrow night, so I won't have to trouble you."

"It's no trouble," Helena assured her politely, but she was inwardly thankful. After what she'd just heard she had the disturbing certainty that Sally was watching her for a reaction. But it was all Alastair's fault, she decided crossly. Bruce should know better than to give that little boy his head in the way he plainly did. In fact—not to put too fine a point on it—everything was Bruce's fault.

She was on edge the whole of next day, trying not to look at Alastair or Sally, but she was horribly conscious of them sitting next to each other. She must find some excuse to separate them, she thought, harassed. Worse still was the feeling that Bruce might suddenly appear. Luckily he didn't.

It was wonderful to get home at last to an empty flat, and be able to relax in the silence. But she found the silence full of the memory of Bruce saying, "your simplistic view of life...," with its disturbing overtones of the way he'd trashed her book: simplified to the point of falsity. At that moment he'd seemed on the verge of discovering her secret, and of all nightmares in the world that one was her worst.

She toyed briefly with the idea of resigning, but she wasn't a quitter. That would be to leave the field to Bruce, and someone must stay to fight for George. He was still in intensive care in the hospital, so ill that she hadn't yet been allowed to see him.

A determined impulse made her pick up the phone and dial the hospital's number. "Can you let me know when it will be possible for me to visit Mr. Fletcher?" she asked for the hundredth time.

"Well—" the nurse on the other end said dubiously, "he's very weak. He should really only be seeing close family for the moment."

"But he doesn't have any close family."

"Oh, yes, his son comes to see him nearly every evening."

"But he—" Helena checked herself. "I'm glad to hear that."

She put the phone down slowly. She knew for a fact that George had never married or had children.

She paced the room restlessly for ten minutes, trying to persuade herself that she was making a fuss about nothing, but she couldn't. Something very strange was going on, and she couldn't rest until she found out what it was. She owed George that after all his kindness to her.

In a moment she was downstairs and running toward the parking lot. Twenty minutes driving took her to the hospital.

She approached the reception desk cautiously. "I've come to see Mr. Fletcher," she said with an air of assurance.

"I'm afraid—"

"I'm his niece," Helena added firmly. "And he's expecting me. I don't want to upset him by not appearing."

"Oh, well, I suppose it'll be all right. He's in room twenty-seven on the third floor. You go down there, take the lift..."

In a couple of minutes Helena was going up in the lift. She reached the third floor, and managed to find room twenty-seven without having to answer any awkward questions. But outside the glass-paneled door she paused, suddenly filled with doubt. Had she done the right thing by coming?

Suddenly she heard George's unmistakable voice through the glass, and the sound of another man answering him. Taking a deep breath, she opened the door.

Then she stopped in her tracks.

George was lying half propped up on pillows. His head was turned toward a man who was sitting by the bed with his back to the door. Helena's heart sank as she realized she'd made a terrible mistake. She couldn't see the visitor clearly, but he was holding one of George's frail hands in both his young, strong ones. His whole attitude radiated comfort and affection, and it was reflected in the face of the invalid whose eyes were fixed on him. Despite the pallor and weary look, George was smiling contentedly, and his face was full of deep affection. There could be no doubt that this young man was his son.

She began to back out quietly, but George happened to glance in her direction and his face lit up. "Look who's here!" he exclaimed happily. "Come in, my dear."

"George, I'm sorry I—I shouldn't be here—"

"Come in, come in. How nice to have the two of you here together."

Then the young man by the bed turned, and Helena saw who it was.

"B-Bruce," she stammered. "I don't understand. What are you doing here?"

"He visits me almost every night," George said. "Now come and give me a kiss."

Helena hurried to embrace him, her head in a whirl. Bruce hadn't said anything, but his expression was quizzical.

"It does my heart good to see you," George told her warmly.

"I'd have come before but they said only close family," she assured him. "They told me only your son was allowed to see you, but I was sure you had no son. Oh, I'm confused. I don't understand anything."

"There are more things in heaven and earth..." Bruce murmured. "I said that to you once before, on the day we met, remember?"

To her own annoyance she blushed. "You may have said something of the kind but I don't see—"

"I also told you about a schoolmaster who saved my sanity by letting me work at my own pace."

"You mean, George—?"

"Of course. He's been a second father to me," Bruce informed her. "I owe him more than I can ever repay, but I'm trying to repay some of it."

Helena let out her breath slowly. "Do you mean—?"

"A few of the governors would like to get me out of Edenbrook," George said. "They want to put some ghastly modernist in, full of meaningless psycho-babble. All style and no substance. Everything I've worked to build up would have been ruined in no time.

"My heart attack could have been their chance. Luckily it happened while I was spending the weekend with the chairman of the governors, who's on my side. Just before I blacked out, I made him promise to contact Bruce and to twist the arm of everyone on the board to get Bruce appointed to hold the fort until I could come back." He chuckled and gripped Bruce's hand. "He had to twist your arm, too, didn't he?"

Bruce grinned. "Not at all. I jumped at the chance to give you something back, you know that."

"I know you're one of life's rovers, always with your eyes on the next horizon. And now I've tied you down..." His voice became suddenly anxious. "But it won't be for long, I promise. I'll be back in no time."

"Of course you will," Bruce told him warmly. "And don't worry. I'll stay, however long it takes."

Helena wished the earth could open and swallow her up. She'd jumped to conclusions and made a fool of herself. But that thought was swept away by wonder as she watched Bruce comforting the old man. There was a gentleness about him that made something catch in her throat.

It seemed so obvious now that being a headmaster didn't suit his style of brilliance and never could. Yet he'd bowed his neck to the yoke to repay a debt of love. That was the kind of man he was.

Then she began to wonder what other kind of man he was, and how much pleasure there would be in finding out. And a curious delight began to steal all over her, spreading until it reached her fingertips and toes. She clutched her hands together, fearful lest she might tremble and betray her thoughts.

"Helena," George's voice brought her out of her reverie. He chuckled at the sight of her face. "You were a million miles away," he said. "What were you dreaming about?"

"Nothing—I—nothing," she said hastily. "Tell me about yourself. How are they treating you in here?"

George made a face. "Like an invalid," he complained.

"You *are* an invalid," Bruce pointed out, grinning.

"Yes, and I'm likely to stay one if I don't get a brandy and soda soon. You don't think—?"

"*No,*" they said together.

He sighed. "Well, it was worth a try. This place is worse than being in the army, except that the sergeant major is a woman. She's insanely cheerful and goes about saying things like, 'Now, Mr. Fletcher, we mustn't upset ourselves, must we?' I told her I'd upset myself if I wanted to. She could do as she pleased."

Helena and Bruce choked with laughter.

"The trouble with you is, you're so used to giving orders, you don't know how to take them," Helena chided him.

"I never gave orders," George protested in an ill-used voice. "I merely asked people in the nicest possible way. That woman doesn't know about asking people nicely. She missed her vocation as a nurse. She should have been a prison commandant."

"Now, Mr. Fletcher, that's quite enough," came a pleasant voice from the door. It belonged to a pretty young woman in a nurse's uniform. From George's guilty reaction there was no doubt that this was the dragon he'd been maligning, and equally no doubt that she'd heard it all before, for she was smiling indulgently.

As she bustled forward to attend to her patient and he received her ministrations with loud complaints that she completely ignored, Bruce and Helena's eyes met, each recognizing in the other the same expression of unholy glee. Their glances locked. The room, and the others in it, faded. Amusement faded, replaced by a sudden, fierce mutual awareness, heavy with the memories of everything that had ever happened between them. Helena's heart began to beat and for a moment she couldn't breathe. She was the first to look away, afflicted by an inexplicable shyness.

"You shouldn't have more than one visitor at a time," the nurse was saying. "But since you look better I'll turn a blind eye this time."

"That's the first sensible thing you've said," George informed her defiantly. "Three cups of tea, please."

The nurse laughed and departed, reappearing a moment later with a tray bearing a pot and three cups. When she'd gone, George said, "Helena, will you be 'mother'?"

"Are you allowed any sugar?" she asked.

"Yes," George insisted.

"No," Bruce said at the same moment.

"No sugar," Helena murmured as she poured.

"He can have a biscuit," Bruce informed her. "One of those dry ones."

George sulked. But he brightened up when Helena handed him his cup, and began to tell funny stories about the hospital routine. It was strangely cozy to be sitting there drinking tea and laughing. Just like a family, Helena thought. She tried to recall the family teas with her uncle and aunt, but they'd lacked the warmth and cheeriness of the present gathering. *This* was what a family should be like.

"And now tell me everything that's happening at school," George demanded of Helena. "What kind of headmaster does he make?"

"Unorthodox," she replied at once. "Just like you, now that I come to think of it." She knew she'd made the right answer when George sighed contentedly. She searched her mind for light gossip that would entertain without worrying him and managed to keep up a steady stream of chat that kept a smile on his face. But she was talking from the top layer of her mind. At a deeper level she was overwhelmingly conscious of Bruce's eyes on her, with a look that they had never had before. It was a warm look that seemed to reach out and enfold her in friendly arms. For the moment passion was in abeyance, but his heart was open to her. She could look inside it and see kindness and chivalry, generosity and understanding. And she loved what she saw.

The nurse appeared in the doorway. "I'm afraid you must go now," she said. "He tires easily."

"Nonsense," George insisted with a last attempt at defiance. "Not a bit...tired—" His eyelids were dropping.

Helena leaned down and kissed him on the cheek, and, to her surprise, Bruce did the same thing, quite naturally. He squeezed George's hand and said, "I'll be back soon."

Then he took Helena's arm and led her quietly from the room.

Chapter Eight

They left the hospital together. As they reached the bottom of the steps, Bruce said tentatively, "Dare I ask you to join me for a cup of tea?"

"My treat," she said, smiling.

They found an old-world tea shop nearby and ordered hot buttered toast and tea. Bruce dug in ravenously. "When did you last eat?" she asked.

"Breakfast. I had to miss lunch because of a meeting, and I can't eat before I visit George because it cuts the time too short, and he frets."

"And then you go home and start work on papers," she said. "It's a heavy load, and you'll make it worse if you get indigestion."

"You've seen how he is. What else do you suggest I do?"

"Nothing. You can't let him down."

He tried to say something, but his mouth was full of toast and it came out as a mumble. She smiled and fell silent. She was filled with transcendent happiness. He wasn't the cold-hearted schemer of her fears. How could she ever have thought that?

She summoned the waitress. "Do you have anything more filling than toast?" she asked.

"Egg and chips, bacon and chips, sausage and chips—" the waitress intoned.

"I want one plate of egg and chips, and one with everything on it, piled high for a starving man."

"Wonderful woman," Bruce growled as the waitress walked away. "But you must let me pay."

"I won't hear of it. I've got to say sorry somehow."

He shook his head. "You've got nothing to be sorry for."

"But I have. I've been misjudging you all this time. I thought you were stealing George's job. I should have known better. It really is tying you down, isn't it?"

He nodded. "I prefer to fly free. I thought once that you knew the truth—when you said I was just holding the fort for him. You could have meant it in one of two ways, so I was very careful how I replied."

"Why didn't you just tell me what was going on?"

"Because I promised George I wouldn't tell anyone. He's afraid of the truth getting out in case his enemies on the school board make a move."

The waitress placed their plates before them and Bruce dug in. Helena fell silent to give him a chance to eat.

"Why are you smiling to yourself in that way?" Bruce demanded suddenly.

"What way?"

"As though you were enjoying a secret. Won't you share it with me?"

"I was just thinking that Alastair would be very disappointed with you. Isn't Sagittarius supposed to be the seeker of truth?"

"Yes. And so?"

"Well, wasn't it a lie when you told the hospital George was your father?"

But Bruce shook his head. "Not even a small white one," he said seriously. "George *is* my father—my spiritual father. There's more than one kind of father, just as there's more than one kind of truth."

He met her eyes as he said it, and something in his gaze made her color. "Don't talk," she said quickly. "Eat it while it's hot."

He dug in gratefully. He knew why she'd changed the subject. There was so much to be said, and so much that they weren't ready to say. They each needed time. "You really thought I wanted George's job," he said. "Was that why you were glaring at me the first day?"

"Yes. I was ready to believe everything bad about you."

"That was very obvious," he said with a grin. "But then things seemed to be going all right—until you suddenly turned against me after we went to that nightclub. Were you feeling guilty about George?"

"No, that was . . . something else."

He watched entranced as the color came and went in her cheeks. Then hunger reclaimed him and he returned his attention to his plate. "That's better," he said at last. He smiled and took her hand. "I feel as though we've just met and I want to know all about you. We said something like that before, didn't we, in the nightclub?''

"I forget exactly what we said," she hedged. The words of that night seemed very dangerous now.

"We wondered whether to go on from where we were, or from where we would normally be after so short an acquaintance."

"But it didn't work out," she recalled. "There was something false about that evening. It could never have worked, except for a short time. Let's start again as strangers, with all the misunderstandings wiped out."

His eyes told her that they could never be entirely strangers, but he didn't say the words. It was enough that they both knew the truth. "We'll begin at the beginning," he agreed, nodding. "I want you to tell me the things you were supposed to tell me that night, about the lift, and why you were scared. I promised you a brotherly evening, and it became—something else. But I promise to be brotherly tonight. Tell me about it. I'll just listen."

There was a little impulse of disappointment at the thought of him being only brotherly, but she suppressed it and said, "Perhaps if I'd been able to talk to someone then, I wouldn't have gone on being scared."

"What happened?" he asked sympathetically. "Did you get stuck in a jammed lift?"

"It wasn't jammed. I was on a school outing to a museum, and when we got into the lift it shot right up to the top of the building, and kept trying to go on up. It rammed the roof again and again, and I was sure it would go through. People were screaming all around me, but I just froze, too terrified to make a sound."

"Dear God!" he breathed. "How old were you?"

"Eight."

"What happened in the end?"

"Someone managed to get through on the emergency phone and the electricity was switched off. It took them an hour to wind us down to the ground."

"Didn't your mother help you get through it?"

"My mother died when I was four. After that I lived with my Aunt Eliza and Uncle James, who had no children of their own."

He heard the constraint in her voice and said, "Weren't you happy with them? Were they unkind?"

"Oh, no. They tried to be good to me, and I think in their way they were fond of me. But they were never demonstrative, and their way of dealing with unpleasantness was to ignore it. Aunt Eliza wouldn't let me talk about what happened in the lift. If I tried, she'd say, 'Just forget about it. It isn't healthy to dwell on things.'"

Bruce groaned and dropped his head into his hands. "So you never got to deal with it at all?" he said after a while.

"Never. And of course I brooded on it and got more afraid until I could hardly bear to step into a lift. That was when I decided I had to get the better of my fear before it completely dominated my life."

"And I brought all the nightmares back. Idiot! Insensitive oaf! I ought to be shot."

"That's going a little far," she said, smiling. "Remind me to kick your shins sometime." They laughed together.

"Tell me more about the lift," he said seriously. "Tell me everything."

So she did. She went into every detail of her feelings, then and since, and he listened to it all with rapt
attention. As she talked she was aware of a new
warmth and peace enveloping her, as though Bruce
were chasing the shadows away. It was different from
the powerful erotic excitement he'd invoked in her that
other night, but no less sweet.

"It's remarkable that you survived as well-balanced
as you are," he observed. "Your file is very impressive. You seem to have sailed through your school days
notching up one success after another with the great-
est ease."

"Oh, no, it wasn't like that," she admitted with an
unconscious sigh. "I got those marks because I
worked my heart out. I didn't have a photographic
memory, as Alastair seems to—and you, too, probably. I learned things and forgot them, and learned
them again—until they stuck."

"It sounds like pure slog," he said sympathetically.

"Most of it was."

Bruce became alert. He wanted to know everything
about her. "But why?" he asked. "What was driving
you? Ambition? Competitiveness?"

"Not really. I worked hard because I wanted to
please my uncle and aunt. But I never got it quite
right."

She was unconscious of the slightly forlorn note in
her voice as she said the last words, but Bruce heard
it, and it made him want to reach out and softly brush
her cheek. He restrained the impulse because he didn't
want to attract attention, but he was aware of new,
confusing feelings stirring within him. Helena was
normally so brisk and capable that this sudden glimpse

of her vulnerability caught him off guard. Something seemed to be hurting in his chest.

"You mean, as hard as you worked they pushed for more?" he asked gently. "That's terrible."

"I'm surprised to hear you say that. What about Alastair?"

"I *never* push him," Bruce said quickly. "I just refuse to hold him back when he wants to race ahead. It's his decision. But we were talking about you. What did your uncle and aunt want from you?"

"Nothing," Helena said, considering. "That was just the trouble. They were doing their duty by me, but I didn't have anything they wanted. I never felt I could bring them any happiness. They didn't push me to get good exam results. I don't think they believed it mattered much. I was the one who did the pushing. I wanted to make them sit up and notice me, but they never did. Not in the way I wanted. I hoped—" She stopped quickly, agitated by the realization that she'd been about tell tell him about her book.

"Hoped what?" Bruce asked, looking at her closely.

"Nothing."

"Tell me, Helena, please."

There was a gentle, caressing note in his voice that she found hard to resist. But this was the one thing she could never tell him, and the fact that she'd been lured so close to the edge was a warning that things weren't as simple as they were trying to pretend. "It's nothing important," she insisted. "It all sounds rather silly now."

"No, it doesn't," Bruce said quickly. "It sounds like one of the saddest things I ever heard. My own childhood seems idyllic by contrast."

"Tell me about it," she said, glad to get off the subject of herself. "I know you've got a sister, because of Alastair. Are there any other brothers and sisters?"

"Just one brother. He went into the church, like my father and grandfather."

"You come from a family of clergy?" Helena couldn't keep the surprise out of her voice, and Bruce glared at her in mock annoyance.

"However unlikely it sounds, yes, I do," he retorted. "I grew up in one of those huge, inconvenient old church houses, full of echoing rooms, long mysterious corridors, and drafts. Half my childhood was dominated by the fight with the church authorities to make them install central heating."

"But you said it was idyllic," Helena reminded him.

"It was. We had a large garden, which was usually unkempt because the man who was supposed to keep it tidy always had an attack of 'rheumatics' whenever there was any hard work to be done. It was a marvelous place for kids to play. There was an orchard and a fat old pony, and what more does any child need?"

"Nothing," Helena said, wistfully picturing the scene. "The church seems to be a family tradition," she observed. "I wonder you didn't go that way, too."

"At one time I was expected to, but that idea didn't last long. I was a bit of a free spirit. I couldn't see a rule without wanting to break it. I had to do everything my own way, or not at all. My father, a man of saintly patience and understanding, said he thought perhaps I shouldn't go into the church. He didn't think the church could stand it."

They both laughed, and Helena said, "I don't think you've changed. I think you're still a free spirit."

"According to that chart Alastair made I'll be a free spirit to the end of my days. What I mostly flee from is responsibility."

"Of course you do," she teased, adding with a mocking inflection, "Headmaster."

He sighed. "It really is very hard for me to do that job. It's everything I hate. Not just the routine—although I find that a terrible burden. It's having to be always accountable to someone. You've no idea how many people there are who can demand an explanation from me. I want to tell them to get off my back and mind their own business. But then I remember that it *is* their business. And that's the hardest of all."

"But nobody can live without ever having to be accountable to someone," Helena said with a frown.

"No, but they can minimize it, and I try to. Alastair would say that makes me a true Sagittarian. Freedom is everything—that's my motto."

"Hence all those narrow escapes from ladies?" Helena said with a twinkle.

He colored. "Something like that. Hell, I'm not really as conceited as it makes me sound. At least, I hope I'm not. I've never believed I was the answer to the maiden's prayer—"

"Well, that would depend on what you thought she was praying for," Helena pointed out impishly.

He grinned. "I don't think any of them really wanted me for keeps, anyway. At heart they all had a bedrock of common sense that warned them what a terrible husband I'd make. And I really would. She'd only have to ask innocently, 'Where have you been, darling?' and I'd feel I was being interrogated. And the fact that she'd actually have the right to ask would make me resent it more.

"I'd turn into a monster, and they know that. But there's something about a freedom-loving man that acts like a red rag to a bull with a woman. He's a challenge. She doesn't want to marry him, she wants to make him admit defeat. If he really got down on one knee proffering a diamond ring, she'd say thank you very much but she was going to marry Fred Faithful who lived next door and had been proposing to her for the last six months."

Helena knew that beneath the comedy Bruce was telling her something serious about himself. They didn't know yet what the feeling between them would turn out to be. It might be a passing fancy, or a love that was deep and true. But whatever the answer, he wasn't a marrying man. To him, marriage just meant more ties.

But the warning didn't depress her because tonight nothing could do that. She was giddy with joy at being reunited with him, and the certainty that being with this man was right. The future could take care of itself, and if there were problems, she would worry about them when the time came. So she just smiled and said lightly, "Personally I'm not a scalp hunter. I'd hate a man to feel he had to be something he wasn't, just because of me. Who wants it? What's the point?"

She had her reward when he lifted her hand and brushed his lips against her fingertips. Heady with success, she continued, "My own freedom means just as much to me, but then you probably know that—after those charts Alastair drew up."

"Have you had a proper look at them? Did Sally—?"

"No, she hasn't shown them to me. She has too much sense of self-preservation. But Leo's also supposed to be a freedom-loving sign. That's why it goes so well with Sagittarius. If Alastair's charts didn't tell you that, *Heavenly Conjunctions* certainly did."

He looked up quickly. "What do you know about that book?"

"Only that you were reading it and spilt coffee on it, right on the significant page." She laughed at the sight of his horrified face. "I got that from Sally, who got it from Alastair, who got it from the stars."

"Is nothing secret from that mad midget?" he asked wildly.

"Nothing to do with us, obviously. I read it when I got home from the nightclub. You'd spilt coffee over the bit where it said I'd be the perfect undemanding playmate, and since that's roughly how the evening had gone I naturally thought—"

He groaned. "Helena, I swear to you, you've misjudged me. If you hadn't been wearing that perfume—the one Sally sprayed over you—it just sort of misled me. I wasn't being calculating."

"Well, I guess I know that now."

"I suppose Alastair means well. I just wish he'd leave me to do my own romancing."

"Perhaps he didn't think you were doing it very cleverly," she pointed out.

"And perhaps he's got a point." Bruce looked at her sitting across from him. It was so right, so natural to be here with her. She was perfect, not only in her beauty but in her sweet understanding of what his freedom meant to him. "There's so much I want to say to you," he told her softly. "But not here. Not now."

She nodded in total comprehension, and he said quickly, "Let's go."

Helena paid the bill and in another moment they were out of the tea shop. As they reached the semi-darkness of the parking lot Helena began to laugh. "What is it?" Bruce demanded. "Come on, tell me."

"George's face when he saw the nurse in the doorway," she chuckled.

Bruce began to laugh, too. "Just like a guilty schoolboy," he said.

His arm was around her shoulders, and somehow her own arm had found its way around his waist, and they stood together, shaking in companionable mirth.

And then suddenly everything changed. His arm tightened, drawing her close to him, his mouth was on hers, and camaraderie disappeared, swamped by passion. Helena's free hand curved instinctively around his head, fingers in his hair, caressing him with joy. She'd missed him so much, and there hadn't been a moment in their estrangement when she hadn't remembered the feel of his lips on hers, and longed to experience it again.

Now it was all being given back to her thousand-fold, and she responded with all her heart. The urgent pressure of his lips told her it was the same with him. Whatever words could say was nothing compared to the powerful message being conveyed by his body as he enfolded her in his arms and took possession of her willing mouth.

She heard him say her name, and the sound mingled with his own name on her lips. Then his tongue was in her mouth, seeking and finding beauty. She gasped and clung to him, drowning in waves of sensuous delight. How could she have lived so long without this man? How could she have endured the last few weeks at odds with him? His lightest touch could open doors of love and delight for her. Knowing that, and fearing it, she had avoided him. But now she wanted to take him and give everything in return.

Yet even in the depths of her joy she felt a small reservation. She loved and wanted Bruce with a completeness that she guessed would frighten him if he knew. The light ribbons of love with which she would gladly have enfolded him would seem like heavy chains tying him down, denying his freedom.

So for the moment she must dissemble, pretending to less than she felt, until the day might come when she could open her heart to him, and he would be ready for what she had to offer. For now she could only give herself up to the sweetness of his embrace, and breathe a silent prayer that that glorious day might dawn soon.

Chapter Nine

When she looked back on that time Helena could only remember details with difficulty. Her chief impression was of happiness, of a world turning to the gold of summer in harmony with her ripening love. Now she could see into his heart and mind and she found them both generous and lovable. Bruce opened a new world to her, not only widening her horizons but showing her to herself anew.

Even her teaching changed, grew deeper and more charged with understanding. She discovered this when she and her class returned to the subject of Queen Elizabeth the first. "Why didn't she marry the Earl of Leicester," sighed one romantic little girl, "if she was so much in love with him?"

"She didn't dare," Helena told her. "Some people suspected he might have killed his wife. He was officially cleared, but if Elizabeth had married him it would still have caused a scandal. So she never married at all, but she didn't stop loving him. When he died she was an old woman, and she treasured his last letter for the rest of her life.''

She'd told the story many times before, but never until now had she fully comprehended the loneliness of the woman who'd been unable to marry the only man she ever loved. Somehow the lesson turned into a debate on the rival claims of love and duty, and several pupils afterward confided in her that it was the most interesting hour they'd ever spent in school.

She went home that night, thoughtful. She was in love with Bruce, and her heart told her that he loved her. But he was no closer to committing himself to her than he had ever been. She resolutely pushed the thought away. It was early days yet. The fear that she might end up lonely and single through losing the only man she could ever love was no more than a tiny cloud on her horizon.

Because of the need to maintain a professional aspect at work, Bruce and Helena tended to see little of each other during the week. The weekends were their time, and they always began with dinner on Friday night. Now that Bruce was able to admit to her how much he disliked being a headmaster he could also work off the strain of his responsibilities by talking out his problems. He would spend much of the dinner in what he called a ''banging my head against the wall'' session in which he complained bitterly about the endless meetings and useless talk, ''which takes three hours to settle something I could have decided myself in ten seconds.'' She listened sympathetically, knowing that was all he needed, and afterward he felt better.

Another of his ways of releasing tension was to entertain her with a stream of amusing chatter about the people he'd known and, more often than not, offended. She found that, although he was a kindly man, Bruce had an uncompromising strain of intellectual arrogance. His comments on some of his learned colleagues were often blisteringly frank. Helena knew him to be generous and incapable of pettiness. He had a sincere admiration for a man who had snatched one of Oxford University's glittering prizes from under his nose. "Perfectly fair. He was, and *is* better than me," Bruce had said simply. But where he detected falseness, unsound thinking, or reputation built on showmanship instead of learning, he was merciless. She knew he wasn't intentionally cruel. He simply couldn't lower his standards, for himself or anybody else. The knowledge prevented her ever confiding in him about her book.

One Thursday he broke their rule about not seeking each other out on school premises, by falling into step with her at the start of the lunchbreak. "I'm afraid we can't see each other this Saturday," he said. "In a weak moment I agreed to appear on *In My Opinion*, and now I can't get out of it."

"Stop pretending to be modest," she chided him. "*In My Opinion* is one of the few really intelligent TV talk shows, and you know it."

"Ah, but you mustn't call it a talk show," he said satirically. "The producer drummed that into me. It's a discussion program, and we're none of us allowed to forget it."

"What's the difference?" she asked with a laugh.

"A talk show is all showbiz, plugs for sex 'n sin autobiographies and backstage gossip dished up by people who are famous for being famous. It goes out at peak time to an audience of millions. A discussion program has panelists who aren't famous for anything—not even for being famous—tackles the great, burning issues of the day, goes out at midnight and is watched by about ten insomniacs, plus a witches coven of journalists hoping a government minister is going to say something he can be made to regret."

Helena chuckled in delight. "You can cut it down if you like," she chided him, "but it's still known as the show that serious people take seriously, and it's a great honor to be invited."

"The producer thinks so, too. That's why he's paying me peanuts. But I resent it because it will take me away from you."

"Never mind. I'll sit at home and watch."

His brow lightened. "But why should you watch at home? Come with me and sit in the audience. Now I think of it, I'm entitled to take a guest."

"That would be lovely."

"We record in the afternoon for transmission that evening. Give me a moment." He returned to his office and joined her on the grounds a few minutes later. "It's all set. We'll meet for lunch on Saturday, and drive to the studio after that."

They arrived in the middle of Saturday afternoon. Bruce was instantly at home, greeting the producer and the floor manager as old friends. Two of the other panelists were already there. One, a woman, was a member of the government, and the other, an elderly man, was an archaeologist with a starry reputation.

"We're still one short," said Dave, the producer. "We're just going to do a quick run-through of the procedure, and the audience will start to arrive in an hour. Would everyone who's here as a guest of a panelist please go and sit over there and be the audience for the run-through?''

The three guests spread themselves out through the hundred seats that had been set on a steep slope. The chairman appeared and the guests clapped like mad in obedience to a signal from the floor manager.

"Good evening and welcome to *In My Opinion*," intoned the chairman with practiced sincerity. "With us tonight..." He introduced the panelists one by one, and the guests clapped each one. "Our last panelist is a publisher, well known for his willingness to take risks with uncommercial subjects for the sake of his beliefs. Please welcome Gordon Frere—only he's not here yet."

"He'll be along any minute," Dave called. "Just let's check the lighting."

Helena sat frozen. Gordon Frere was going to be here. Gordon Frere, who had published her book on Darwin, who knew her secret, who could give her away to Bruce without even meaning to. Only last night, over dinner, Bruce had been talking about "slipshod, showy pseudo academics who use hype to replace original thought." Now she was on the verge of being revealed as one of them. Oh, this couldn't be happening!

"Right, that's fine!" Dave called. "Thank you, everyone. Now, if you'd all like to come along to the hospitality suite, we have half an hour to relax."

Bruce came to fetch her. "Are you all right, darling?" he asked anxiously. "You look strange suddenly."

"I do feel a little odd," she said, seeing a glimmer of hope. "Perhaps I should go away—"

"Come along and I'll get you a brandy. That'll pick you up."

His arm was around her, guiding her inexorably toward the hospitality suite. In a few moments they were there. Seats were dotted around the wall and there was a long, white-covered table at one end of the room. Behind it waitresses dispensed food and drink to a crowd of people, for the suite served several programs and was already full of guests. "Sit down and I'll get you something," Bruce said tenderly, guiding her to a seat.

"Not brandy. I hate it."

"A nice cup of tea, then? Do you have anything you can take?"

"N-no—y-yes—I don't kn-know—" she stammered, not knowing what she was saying.

"My poor dear. What a rotten thing to happen. Stay here."

While he was gone she sat thinking wildly to find a way of escape. But the next moment she looked up to see Gordon Frere standing in the doorway, looking around him. She felt a surge of relief and joy that she still had a chance of escape, and raised a hand to attract his attention. He saw her, smiled and came over. He was a tall man in his early forties, with looks that many women considered handsome, although the only time he'd made Helena's heart beat faster was when he'd accepted her book.

"How nice to see you, sweetie," he said, smiling and bestowing on her the meaningless endearment she'd heard him give to every woman he encountered.

"Gordon, I haven't much time. Sit by me, quickly."
She almost pulled him down onto the seat beside her.
"I've never told anyone about my book, and I want it
to stay that way. Promise you won't give me away,
please."

"All right, if that's how you want it. But I don't see
why you—"

"Just promise," she commanded fiercely.

"I promise. It's all in the past."

"No, it isn't. It didn't happen at all," she insisted.

"If you say so. Anyway, the future's more interesting, sweetie. I've been meaning to call you and ask if
you'd care for another try. We could find a subject
that suits you better and—"

"It's nice of you to have faith in me, Gordon, but
no thank you. I'll never write another book. But, oh,
I can't tell you what it means to me to have your
promise."

Relief was making her feel almost faint, and she was
aware that a big foolish smile had overtaken her face.
She couldn't help it. A moment ago the world had
been dark and now the sun was shining again.

There was a crowd at the buffet, forcing Bruce to
cool his heels for a while. To pass the time he glanced
around the room, and saw a tall, good-looking man
enter and pause a moment in the doorway.

Then, as Bruce watched, an incredible thing happened. Helena looked up and saw the newcomer. At
once she seemed to come alive and she signaled urgently to catch his attention. As he noticed her, a smile
of recognition spread over his face and he went directly over to where she was sitting. Helena reached up

to take both his hands in hers and drew him down to sit beside her.

Bruce stayed motionless watching them. Helena was saying something very urgently. The man was nodding and smiling. The sound of conversation in the room rose and faded just enough for Bruce to pick up the odd word. He was speaking now, saying words Bruce could only half hear. "The future's more interesting, sweetie...meaning to call you...another try...we could find a..."

Bruce became aware that a waitress was tugging at his sleeve. "You were miles away," she told him. "What can I get you?"

"A pound of arsenic," Bruce growled, with his eyes on Helena's companion.

"*What?*"

"Nothing. Just a joke. A cup of tea please—and a very stiff whiskey."

Just who the hell did this man think he was to call her sweetie?

He approached them, his face bearing a creditable imitation of an affable smile. "Your tea," he said, handing Helena a cup.

He had a shock when she looked up. Her pallor had gone. A moment ago she'd seemed on the verge of fainting. Now she looked brimming with health and good cheer. "I don't believe we've met?" he said coolly to the man.

"Oh—this is Gordon Frere," Helena said awkwardly. "Gordon, Bruce Venables."

The two men exchanged unenthusiastic greetings. "I have to go now," Frere said. "I see Dave trying to get my attention. 'Bye, sweetie."

He departed and Bruce claimed the vacant chair. "How nice for you to find an old friend," he said.

"Oh, but he isn't," Helena said hastily. "That is, I hardly know him—just to say hello to."

It occurred to Bruce that she hadn't greeted Frere like a man she hardly knew, but clearly she didn't realize he'd seen her. It also occurred to him that he was becoming agitated about nothing.

No, it wasn't nothing. She knew Frere far better than she admitted, which meant she'd lied to him, and a woman only lied to a man about another man for one reason. This Frere person was a past romance— and not so far past, either, if her joy at seeing him was anything to go by. An unfamiliar malaise was gripping Bruce. It wasn't like the possessiveness that had seized him in the nightclub. That had been disconcerting but pleasurable because she'd been undoubtedly his and the other men had been outsiders. Now, suddenly, he was the outsider while another man fanned the flames of an old fire in the woman he loved, and he didn't like it. He sat there, dazed, trying to come to terms with the most violent attack of jealousy of his entire life.

He'd been jealous before, so he'd thought. Women had teased him with other flirtations, some of which had troubled him. He'd been rather proud of his ability to cope with an emotion that he despised as uncivilized. He'd behaved rationally, and he and the ladies were still friends.

Now he realized that he'd coped so well because he hadn't really cared. What he'd taken for the authentic green-eyed monster had been no more than a feeling of being slightly miffed. True jealousy was this churning, gut-gripping, black-walled misery that was invading him, reducing his brilliant intelligence to jelly. Jealousy was something that punched him in the stomach because the special woman had given another man a smile with a world of meaning that excluded himself. Jealousy was the hell he'd found himself in when she pretended the other relationship didn't exist and he knew she was lying.

From a great distance he heard Dave's voice calling everyone into the studio. "We'd better go," Helena said. "It looks like the program is about to begin." She laid a solicitous hand on his arm. "Are you all right, darling?"

Look at her, he thought frantically, smiling as if nothing had happened, looking so beautiful and sincere, while all the while she was deceiving him with another man. *Jezebel.*

"I'm fine," he said abruptly, taking a swallow of the whiskey.

"Are you wise to drink that just before the program?" she asked with a frown.

Bruce gritted his teeth. "I need it." He threw back his head and tossed off the rest with one gulp.

"Ready?" Dave said at his elbow. "Let's have a great show with all the panelists carving each other up."

"Suits me," Bruce said with deadly cheerfulness. "I'm in the mood to eat lions."

Without another word, he strode off to the studio with a smile frozen onto his face, whiskey curdling in his stomach and murder breeding in his heart.

Any fear he'd had that his wits might be addled was soon dissipated. No sooner had the program started than his head cleared, and from then on he was in sparkling form. What followed was one of the liveliest exchanges that had ever taken place on this program. It soon became apparent that there were really only two protagonists. The government minister and the distinguished archaeologist faded into the background while Bruce Venables and Gordon Frere slogged it out.

Whatever the topic under discussion, they were on different sides, expressing their disdain for each other in words of icy courtesy. Bruce would listen to his rival's opinions with a smile of lofty amusement before protesting, "No, really I can't let you get away with that. We both know it's the most errant nonsense."

It was said in the mildest of voices, but by the restrained standards of academic debate, Bruce was putting the boot in, and everybody there knew it. What was more, they loved it. The audience cheered them both on like gladiators, indifferent to who was winning as long as there was a thrilling fight. Bruce felt his wounded ego recovering, although he knew he was behaving irrationally and with a disregard for strict truth that was shocking. He was arguing against propositions he agreed with simply to score points off Gordon Frere. It was true that Frere was thick-skinned enough to take it and come back, scoring a few points of his own, but Bruce knew that he himself was behaving badly.

Still, he couldn't stop. Primitive exultation filled him as he felt himself grinding to dust the man who had dared challenge him for his woman. He was better at this kind of debate than Frere, having the gift of diffusing acerbic argument with humor. Once when he managed this, the chairman turned to the audience and said, "Is there anybody else who has an opinion on this?"

Helena put up her hand and the camera swung to her. She was still laughing from Bruce's last outburst as she said skeptically, "Surely Mr. Venables doesn't mean that he really believes—?" Bruce barely heard the rest of the question in the shock of realizing that Helena had weighed in against him.

Before he could reply, Frere spoke up. "Of course he believes it. A man whose thinking is as muddled as Mr. Venables has demonstrated today will believe anything."

There was another laugh in which Bruce managed to join. Then the chairman was saying, "Well, that's all we have time for..." And it was over.

The audience was drifting away. The panelists left their podium. Frere seized Bruce's hand and pumped it up and down cheerfully. "Dashed good argument. Never enjoyed myself more. I thought you kept your end up pretty well—considering."

With difficulty Bruce restrained himself from committing violence on Gordon Frere's immaculate person. Helena was there, smiling at Gordon, who was smiling back.

"Bye, sweetie. Nice to see you again. Now I have to rush. Goodbye, Venables."

"Goodbye," Bruce said tightly.

"Well, that was fun," Helena said, slipping her arm into his.

"I'm glad you enjoyed it."

"What's the matter? You sound annoyed."

"Of course I'm not annoyed. Let's go and have something to eat."

She was hungry but the meal was spoiled for her by a tooth that had begun to twinge an hour earlier, and was now rapidly progressing into a full-scale ache. At

last she gave up trying to eat. Bruce, normally so solicitous and tender, noticed nothing. He sat in clouds
of gloom, and when he did speak, it clearly cost him
an effort. Helena wondered if this was simply a nervous reaction after a public performance, but when
she made the suggestion, he simply growled, "Nonsense."

She began to be annoyed with him. She'd looked
forward to today, and now it was being spoiled, both
by his attitude and the toothache. The toothache was
obviously his fault in some obscure way that she
couldn't pin down. After all, if he could be unreasonable, so could she.

On the way home she said, "You *are* annoyed. It's
not like you to be in a bad mood. Come to think of it,
you haven't been like yourself since before the program. You really got your knife stuck into Gordon."

"He's a big boy," Bruce said coldly. "He can take
care of himself."

"Of course. I just wondered why you were having
a go at him."

"I was *not* having a go at him. I was challenging
him to clarify his ill thought out ideas."

"Oh, is that what it's called? It sounded exactly like
having a go at him."

To Bruce's dismay he heard himself becoming
pompous. "To you, possibly. But there's a distinc-
tion to be drawn between verbal brawling and the cut
and thrust of debate."

"Cut and thrust of fiddlesticks! You were having a
go at him."

"If you say that once more—"

"Yes? What? Will you have at go a me? You're dying to, aren't you? You'd love an excuse to take your temper out on me."

"I am not in a temper," he asserted with biting emphasis.

"You are," she snapped. "You're in a filthy temper. I can't think why. You got the best of it, except at the very end."

"Ah, yes, the very end," he said bitterly. "You just couldn't resist sticking your oar in to undermine me, could you?"

"Well, you were talking nonsense. I've heard you say exactly the opposite to what you were saying then. I couldn't believe my ears."

"So you had to make a fool of me in front of him?"

"I didn't make a fool of you. I merely suggested, in the mildest possible way, that what you were saying didn't add up. Is that a crime? Anyway, you're a big boy, aren't you? You can take care of yourself."

"That's hardly the point."

"If it was the point for Gordon, it's the point for you. Honestly, Bruce, you know you'd backed yourself into a corner by saying things you didn't mean. You'd have seen it if you hadn't been so intent of having a g—"

"Don't say it."

"All right, I won't. But it's true and you know it."

A sulphurous silence fell between them. Helena was dismayed at the quarrel but she had less attention for it than she might have done. The tooth was getting worse by the moment. All she longed for was to get home to bed. Nobody spoke until he reached two streets away from her house. "I believe this is where you prefer to get out?" he said coolly.

It was where he normally dropped her in order to avoid the curious eyes of Alastair and Sally, but with the throbbing in her tooth she would have been glad to abandon caution and be taken straight home. A considerate man, she thought crossly, would have known that without being told. He would even have known about her toothache without being told. In fact, she couldn't imagine why she ever wasted her time on someone so self-centered. "Thank you," she said, gathering her things.

"Are we seeing each other tomorrow?" he asked in the same tone.

The tooth throbbed, almost making her gasp. Oh, bed! Oh, hot milk! Oh, aspirin!

"I don't think so," she said. "I have a lot of things to do."

"Fine, so have I."

"Goodbye, then. And thank you for a *delightful* day."

He gave her a furious look and drove off without answering.

Chapter Ten

By next morning he was sorry. He was more than sorry, he was bewildered at himself. How could he have made so much fuss over a trivial matter? He, who despised jealousy? He would call her up today, apologize for his ill temper, and make everything right. Smiling, he dialed her number.

But his smile faded as the ringing went on and on and on. At last he replaced the receiver. So she was out? So what? She was a free woman, entitled to go out without telling him, wasn't she? Just as he was a free man, entitled to go out without telling her.

To prove it, he went out. He didn't want to, but he hoped it might reassure him. He went to his favorite pub, a place where he had often whiled away a relaxing hour on a Sunday morning. He always said you could tell the husbands. They were the ones who started looking at their watches around one o'clock, saying, "Well, just a quick one," then drifting off because Sunday lunch would be on the table and *she* would get cross if it spoiled. Bruce had felt quite superior at having no *she* to dictate what time he returned for lunch. Oh yes, he'd made very merry about husbands. But when he thought of the empty flat awaiting him and the phone that wasn't answered, it suddenly didn't seem so funny anymore.

He strolled home, refusing to walk fast. In the flat he made himself some coffee, not hurrying about it. He would ring her in his own good time. When he felt a dignified interval had passed, he dialed her number again. This time he heard the busy signal. She was probably trying to call him. He waited ten minutes and called again. Still busy. He made a frantic call to the operator who, when she could get a word in edgewise, informed him frostily that there was nothing wrong with the line. After that he abandoned dignity and tried at regular fifteen minute intervals through the afternoon. And whenever he heard the engaged signal, he died a little.

It was obvious what had happened. Helena had gone out to meet Gordon Frere that morning, but their feelings had overcome them and they'd returned to her flat for... for what? What would they be doing that made her take the phone off the hook first? He didn't answer that. He didn't want to. He was scared.

But she's not like that, his other self argued. *She's decent and sweet and honest. That's why you're in love with her.*

So why is the phone off the hook?

Alastair returned from a weekend with his grandparents and Bruce roused himself enough to be pleasant. This was partly conscientiousness and partly an appalled vision of the scientific gleam that would enter Alastair's eye if he got a hint of anything wrong. He managed to be a good uncle until bedtime, but the effort exhausted him. He retired, expecting to collapse into sleep, and stayed awake all night. He hadn't known it was possible to suffer so much.

In the morning he caught a distant sight of her at school assembly, but then she shepherded her class out and vanished. They never spoke to each other at assemblies, but often their glances locked. He'd tried to meet her eyes, but she didn't look at him. He had the feeling that her attention was a hundred miles away.

At midday he looked for her in the dining room, but she wasn't there. He spent another hour wrestling with his pride before giving in and sending Deirdre, a fifth form pupil, with a formal message to Miss Walker that the headmaster would like to see her. Deirdre returned a few minutes later, alone. "I'm sorry, Mr. Venables, but Miss Walker isn't coming back today."

"Coming back? You mean she's left?"

"Somebody called her about two hours ago, and she said she had to go out immediately. She asked Mrs. Kenway to take her classes for the rest of the day."

"You, er, don't happen to know who the call was from?"

"Someone said they thought it was a man, but they didn't know who. Shall I—?"

"No, thank you," he said hastily.

That was it, he told himself wildly. Getting her paramour to call her at school, abandoning her duties to rush off into his arms. Disgraceful! It was his plain duty to put a stop to it.

He informed his secretary that he had to go out, and within a few minutes he was in his car, heading for Helena's home. All the way there he was fighting the urge to turn back. He didn't really want to know. *Don't find out. Don't see it. Wait for it to burn itself out and she comes back to you.* But his passion for the truth blocked off that road. Almost before he knew it, he'd reached her house.

He saw the sports car at once. It was sleek, white and low slung, an elegant sexy vehicle, of the kind Gordon Frere would be bound to own. And it was parked shamelessly right in front of her house.

He almost turned tail and departed, but something made him stop and get out to examine the offending car. He walked around it, then looked up at her window at the very moment one of the curtains was drawn back and Helena's face appeared. The shame of being caught mooning about her home like a lovesick boy made him want to sink out of sight. He stared at her, transfixed, until at last it dawned on him that she was signaling for him to come inside.

She was waiting for him as he reached the top of the stairs, and stood back for him to go inside. There was nobody else there. He studied her properly for the first time, and realized that she looked as if she'd been through the mill. One cheek was slightly swollen, and when she spoke it was with difficulty. "It was sweet of you to come and see how I am, darling. I've been feeling grim."

"You look as if you've had a bad time," he said, choosing his words carefully.

"Rotten. It was an abscess, and my dentist was away over the weekend. Today was the first time he could see me."

Relief poured over him in cascades, making him catch his breath. "So that's why you—I mean, you've been to the dentist?"

"I left a message. Didn't you get it?"

"Only that a ma—that somebody had called you and you'd left."

"I left a full explanation about going to the dentist," she said in dismay.

"The wires must have got crossed. I didn't know what to think when you vanished."

"So you dashed around here to find out if something had happened to me?" Helena's eyes softened and she put her arms around him, resting her head on his shoulder. "You really are nice, Bruce, especially after I was so rotten to you on Saturday. I think you must be the nicest man I ever knew."

Her words had the effect of introducing him to another fresh experience, that of feeling utterly and totally ashamed of himself. Nice? He was a worm. He was lower than a worm. He was the lowest form of life existent. And it would serve him right if she found out about him.

In the same moment he resolved to tell her. She was entitled to squash him beneath her heel before throwing him out. "Don't praise me, darling," he pleaded. "I've got to tell you— Here, sit down and let me look after you. Confessions can come later. Can I get you something?"

"Some hot milk, please."

He made it and brought it out to where she was curled up on the sofa. She drank it down with some aspirin, and looked happier. "When did all this start?" he asked contritely.

"Saturday afternoon. That's really why I bit your head off."

"No, no, I asked for that. It was all my fault."

"Well, anyway, I called my dentist but all I got was his answering machine saying he'd be away until Monday. I left a message and went to bed for the rest of the weekend. Luckily I had something to make me sleep, and I slept right through until the phone woke me on Sunday morning. But by the time I got to it, whoever it was had hung up. After that I took it off the hook so that I wouldn't be disturbed. This morning the dentist called me at school to say I could come at once. So I dashed off. I know I look awful but I'm actually feeling a lot better. Bruce, what's the matter?"

"Oh, Lord," he groaned, sinking his head into his hands. "What a fool I've been!"

"Why?"

"I thought— Well, that'll keep."

"You thought what?"

"Later, when you've completely recovered."

"No, tell me now."

"When you seemed so pleased to see Gordon Frere, I thought—that is, it crossed my mind— Not that I took it seriously—at least, not very seriously—"

"Bruce, I can't follow any of this."

"Doesn't the name 'Gordon Frere' make it any clearer?"

A cautious look came into her eyes. "Not really."

"Oh, come on, darling. It was obvious that you two used to know each other very well, although you tried to hide it. In fact it was your hiding it that first got me worried. If he was just a friend, why not just say so?"

The wary look vanished and an impish smile hovered over her lips, even touching the swollen side. "Are you telling me you were jealous?"

"Of course not—maybe just a little— Hell, *yes!*"

"Bruce, I swear to you, there's never been any romance between me and Gordon. There never could be."

He heaved a sigh of relief. "That's what I kept telling myself. But when I couldn't reach you yesterday I thought you must be with him." A sudden need for movement made him get up and stride about the room. He came to the window just as a smartly dressed man emerged from the neighboring house with a young woman. He proceeded to open the door of the white sports car, usher her in, get into the driver's seat, and drive away. Bruce began to laugh.

"What is it?" Helena asked.

"Nothing. A man's entitled to laugh at his own foolishness." He came and sat beside her, taking her tenderly into his arms. "Promise you're mine and I swear I'll never be a fool again."

"Promise," she said at once.

He kissed her good cheek very gently. "So now tell me about him."

"Who?"

"Gordon Frere."

"But there's nothing to tell."

"There must be. You were overjoyed at seeing him, and he was saying something about the future and—"

"Were you listening?" she asked sharply.

"I—I just happened to pick up a few words," he stammered, alarmed by the glint in her eye. "I was curious, that's all." When she didn't say anything Bruce went on desperately, "If he's just a harmless friend, why the big secret?"

"If I tell you he's just a harmless friend, don't you believe me?"

"Of course, I believe you."

"Then you've no reason to ask me any more, have you?"

"But—"

"Bruce, you're the one who doesn't believe in interrogations. You're the one who thinks people should give each other space. Well, you're invading my space, and I'm asking you—no, I'm *telling* you—to back off, because it's private."

Bruce opened his mouth. Then he shut it again. He'd been protecting his own space, not hers. In fact he hadn't even thought of hers. But it wouldn't be wise to admit that.

There was just no end to the new experiences that could overtake a man in a few short days.

By Thursday she was well enough to be taken to dinner. "To celebrate your recovery," as Bruce put it. She was living in a happy dream since the discovery of his jealousy. Being a warm-hearted man, he described his sufferings for her amusement, and endured her laughter without resentment. She knew that jealousy was against his principles—or at least, so he'd thought—and that his own bout of it had taken him aback, making him look at her with new eyes. Perhaps, she thought, he'd even moved one step further toward that commitment that she longed for.

"You look lovely," he said as he raised his wineglass to her.

"You mean my face is no longer the size of a football?" she teased.

"I mean you look lovely." They clinked the glasses. "Actually, Helena, there's been something I've been meaning to say to you."

"Yes?" she said, trying not to sound eager.

"Term will be over in a few weeks, and we haven't made any plans for seeing each other. I certainly don't want us to spend the summer apart—not now we're so close."

"Neither do I," she agreed, her heart beginning to beat harder.

"Have you ever been to Paris?"

Paris, she thought ecstatically. What a wonderful place for a honeymoon.

"Never," she told him.

"Well I'll be taking the fourth form on a school trip to Paris during the summer holiday. I'll need at least one other staff member to come with me. How about it?"

For a moment she couldn't take it in. "How about what?" she asked in a daze.

"Coming to Paris on the school trip. It'll be mostly hard work, but at least we'll see each other. What do you say? My poor darling, is your tooth hurting you again?"

"How can it hurt me when I've had it out?" she said, more sharply than she'd intended.

"All right. No need to snap at me. I wondered why you looked like that."

"I was just realizing that I don't have a passport," she said wildly, wishing she could tip the wine bottle over his head.

"No problem there. Just get your birth certificate and send it off to the passport office. You'll have to be quick, though. This is the busy time of year."

"Fine," she responded in a colorless voice. "I'll do that."

"It'll be wonderful to see Paris together, won't it?"

"Wonderful!" she echoed hollowly. "You, me and twenty fourth formers all chomping at the bit to get out of the Louvre and into the Folies Bergere. I can't wait."

He grinned. "You know, sometimes I think what I love about you most is your sense of humor."

Over coffee he began to talk about what they would do together on the weekend, and mentioned a beautiful spot he was fond of in the midlands. Helena nodded. "It's at its best this time of year," she told him.

"Do you know that part of the country?"

"I grew up there. My aunt and uncle still live in the town of Havering."

"Great. We'll drive up there, and you can take me to visit them."

"That would be lovely—one day," she said cautiously.

"Why 'one day'? Why not this weekend?"

"I'll have to call and see what they're doing."

"If they're busy this weekend, next weekend will do." Bruce took a look at her anxious face, and his tone changed. "I didn't mean to sound pushy. Do they have very busy lives with every moment counting double?"

"Nothing like that. I'm sure they'll be free," she said hastily.

"What is it, darling? Don't you want me to meet them?"

She thought of the little town that had been her home for several years, of the small supermarket branch where her uncle had been assistant manager for years, doomed never to rise higher. "I wouldn't have got this far, but the ambitious young fellows don't want to live out in the sticks," he'd once said, laughing contentedly.

Helena thought of her aunt with her passion for making everything "nice" and doing things "the proper way." They were decent people and their world had a certain cozy charm. But it was also bound by very narrow horizons, which they never seemed to notice, or if they noticed, they didn't mind.

She recalled her visits home, the strained atmosphere as they all tried to find something to say across the gap of diverse interests. They had nothing in common, and without love to carry them through, the chasm often seemed very wide. But she couldn't explain any of this to Bruce. "I'll call them as soon as I get home," she promised him.

Even so, she hesitated for a long time that night before she actually lifted the receiver and dialed. Aunt Eliza answered. When the ritual greetings had been exchanged, Eliza said, "We saw you on the telly. You were in the audience of some show or other. We only spotted you by accident because we were switching channels to get the weather report before we went to bed, and there you were on the screen. I didn't believe it was you at first. Your uncle said, 'That's Helena,' and I said, 'No, it can't be.' But he said, 'Yes it is,' and I said, 'So it is. That's nice.'"

"Did you watch the rest of the show?" Helena said, thinking this would be a good way to introduce Bruce.

"Not to say watched. We stayed with it to catch another glimpse of you, and we saw when you asked the question at the end. You looked ever so nice. Everyone said so."

"Goodness! Who else watched?"

"Well, naturally I called Mrs. Arnwood." Helena smiled as she recognized the name of Eliza's favorite rival for supremacy in their little community. Plainly Eliza now felt one up.

"What did you think of the speakers on the panel?" she asked cautiously.

"Oh, I didn't notice them. I can never make head nor tail of the things they say on those programs. I prefer a nice game show. We only watched because of you."

"Well, I was only there because one of the speakers invited me as his guest. In fact, I'd like to bring him to visit you this weekend."

"All right, dear. That'll be nice."

"It's not putting you out, is it?"

"No, no. I'll cook something nice."

She told him next day that it was all on. "Great," he said. "Shall I collect you at your home on Saturday morning?"

"Er, no," Helena said hastily. "I'll meet you a couple of streets away, the way I usually do. If you call at the house you know who'll be watching."

"Sally. Yes, of course."

"Don't you ever get the feeling of being under surveillance at home?"

"Alastair knows when it's wise for him to keep quiet. But now you mention it, his silence has had a certain deafening quality recently. Perhaps—"

He checked himself with something like horror. He'd been about to say, "Perhaps we should simply run away and marry quietly." He'd been on the verge of suggesting *marriage.* He'd spent his entire adult life guarding against the "M" word, and it had nearly slipped out before he could stop it.

He knew he hadn't been quite himself since his bout of jealousy. His mind had started wandering into fantasies about finding ways to make her his own forever. Just the same, it was a shock to discover how far out of control his inner self was racing. It had felt so right, so natural, and in another moment the waters would have closed over his head.

"What's the matter?" Helena queried. "You look as if you've swallowed a fly."

"Nothing," he said hastily. "You're quite right. I'll meet you two streets away. I have to be going now." He felt a strong need to put a distance between them until he was in his right mind again.

Sunday was a beautiful early summer day, and Helena knew she looked her best in the thin cotton dress of pale blue. If nothing else had told her that, Bruce's eyes would have done so. He kissed her briefly when she got into the car, then drove for a couple of hours, until they were deep in the midland countryside. When they were within a few minutes of Havering, he stopped the car on the grass verge and said, "Darling, are your uncle and aunt terribly respectable?"

"Terribly," she confessed.

"In that case, I'd better kiss you now, while I have the chance."

He drew her into his arms and her head found its usual place on his shoulder. The sweetness of his lips on hers was a familiar joy by now, yet it still came as a fresh shock every time. If only, she thought, they need go no further, but could stay here loving each other all afternoon. She embraced him back passionately, putting all her love into the kiss, hoping he would understand its message and not take fright. She was happy with Bruce, but sometimes it was tiring to have to remember that she walked a tightrope. Too much love might come to seem like a trap to him, so she held back, longing to let him know everything that was in her heart, yet fearing it, too.

But the silent words of a kiss could say everything, for he could take from it whatever he was ready to hear. His hands were trembling as they held her, and when he drew back, his voice wasn't quite steady.

"This wasn't a good idea," he said. "I don't feel respectable anymore."

"Neither do I," she said recklessly.

"I wish we weren't going to Havering. I want us to just drive off together."

Helena was silent, her heart beating madly with hope.

"I want—I want—" Bruce seemed to be fighting an inner battle. At last he took a deep ragged breath. "I want all sorts of things that I can't have. Let's go before my wits become completely addled."

"Yes," she said with a little sigh. "Let's go."

Chapter Eleven

As they drew closer she realized she was nervous. What would James and Eliza, with their seeming disdain for everything Bruce stood for, make of him? At last she could see the little bungalow with its white walls, green shutters and flowers about the door. How pretty it was, she thought, and how nice it would have been to come home to if only things had been different between herself and her relatives.

As they came closer, the front door opened and her uncle and aunt hurried out, looking eagerly down the road. It was something they hadn't done on her previous visits home. Her surprise deepened as she got out of the car and Eliza came forward and enfolded her in an eager embrace. "Well now, there you are," she said, smiling. "It's good to have you back."

Helena hugged her, warmed and delighted by the pleasure in Eliza's eyes. The next moment she was enfolded in James's arms.

"This is Bruce," she said when she was free, and saw the slight shock on their faces as they recognized him from the screen.

For a moment they seemed a little shy, but then Eliza said, "I've got the kettle on for a nice cup of tea," and Bruce exclaimed, "Just what I was longing for!" and the ice was broken.

Within a few minutes Helena knew that her fears had been groundless. In fact, the visit was a happier experience than she would have dared to hope, mostly because her aunt seemed transformed. Helena couldn't imagine why it had suddenly happened, but several times she caught Eliza looking at her with a fond approval on her face that had never been there before. It was a look she'd dreamed of seeing over the years, but only now did she have her wish. Conscience stricken, she realized how long it had been since she was last here. Perhaps Eliza had missed her. That must be it. It wasn't too late for affection to flow spontaneously between them. In her newfound happiness, Helena gave her aunt an impulsive hug and felt it returned vigorously.

"Well," Eliza said, in a contented voice. "Fancy that now. Just fancy that."

Superficially the words could have meant anything, but to Helena they were confirmation that Eliza's feelings reflected her own.

"When you said you were bringing someone who'd been on that program, I thought you meant the other one, the good-looking one—Gordon Something,"

Eliza said when they were doing odd jobs in the kitchen.

"Bruce is good-looking," Helena objected.

"He is when you see him in the flesh, but the other one's more handsome on telly," Eliza insisted.

"Don't let Bruce hear you say that," Helena warned. "I know Gordon slightly, and somehow Bruce convinced himself that he ought to be jealous. Don't even hint that Gordon's better looking or that'll start him off again."

"Oh, jealous is he?" Eliza queried with a smile. "Is that why he was going for him hammer and tongs?"

Helena chuckled. "Actually it was, although Bruce won't admit it. He got cross with me when I said so, and insisted it was just impersonal academic debate."

The two women laughed together, and Helena felt her cup of happiness running over.

"What does he do, this Bruce of yours?" Eliza asked.

"He's the headmaster at Edenbrook. That's how we met."

"But they don't put ordinary headmasters on telly, do they?" Eliza pointed out.

"No, he's really only filling in until George gets well, and it's quite a sacrifice for him. He's a very distinguished man. He's written dozens of books."

"He must do very well out of it if he can afford that car," Eliza observed placidly.

"Why, what do you know about cars?" Helena said, laughing in surprise.

"Nothing, but your uncle likes to dream about them. He wants one just like that, and he got all the stuff from the manufacturer. When he found out what it cost he nearly fainted. That's how I know.''

Helena was seeing not only Eliza but also Bruce in a new light that afternoon. From the first moment he had seemed completely at home, discussing gardening with James, and responding to a tentative invitation to inspect the soft fruit with an eagerness that seemed entirely genuine. Helena associated Bruce with the trappings of academe, running the school or sitting up into the early hours to finish a book that the Oxford University Press was waiting for. But when she and Eliza wandered out to the greenhouse half an hour later they found the men deep in a discussion of how to avoid greenfly from which they could only be roused with difficulty.

"He knows a lot, that chap," James confided to her as they went back to the house.

Helena remembered what Bruce had told her about his childhood in the old vicarage with the orchard and the fat pony. He fit in here more perfectly than she had dared to hope, she realized.

He proved it when he discovered Uncle James looking at his car out of the window, with longing eyes. A few careful questions elicited the truth, and Bruce immediately suggested a spin. To everyone's amusement James was halfway out of the door before he'd finished.

They drove for half an hour, with James reveling in the smoothness and silence of the engine, and becoming speechless with delight when Bruce invited him to drive. Helena and Eliza sat in the back together, and every so often Eliza would squeeze her hand and throw her a beaming smile. Helena smiled back, puzzled but happy.

When they returned home Eliza indicated with a movement of her head that they should both go into the kitchen. Helena followed her, and Eliza immediately shut the door. "Well?" she said eagerly.

"Well, what?"

"You know. When's it to be?"

"When's what to be?"

"The wedding, of course. You *will* have a nice church wedding, won't you, dear? You'll look so lovely in white."

"Whoa, hold on there. You're running way ahead, Aunt Eliza."

"Am I? Well, it's just a matter of time, isn't it? Anyone can see you two are in love."

"Yes, but that doesn't mean—that is, these days—"

"Nonsense. People can say what they like about things being different, but couples in love still get married, don't they?"

"Some of them do," Helena said slowly. "But not every man is the marrying kind."

"No man is the marrying kind until he finds the right woman," Aunt Eliza said complacently. "She has to *make* him into the marrying kind. That's what I had to do with your uncle."

Helena gave an inward groan as she heard the old saw trotted out as if it was eternal truth. All the social changes of the last few decades might not have happened as far as Eliza was concerned. "Women don't have to get married these days, Auntie."

"Pooh! Stuff and nonsense! That's what they say,
but I know better. Women want what they've always
wanted, a husband and children. Some things don't
change. You've done very well for yourself, dear.
Fancy getting somebody distinguished. But you were
always the clever one."

The truth was becoming horribly clear to Helena.
Her uncle and aunt were narrow, old-fashioned people, still mentally stuck in the time when a woman
proved her worth by finding a good husband. Nothing else counted. Today, in Eliza's eyes, Helena had
finally proven her worth by finding a good "catch."
She couldn't understand that the world had moved on.

As if to prove it, Eliza continued, "Anyway, why
are we talking like this when you've found your man?
I always knew you'd make a good match. You were
the prettiest girl in the school. At least, you were when
I could make you wear a pretty dress, which was almost never. You always preferred running about in
jeans and climbing trees. I could never see the point of
your wasting your time on those dull old exams. But
there! You wouldn't have met him if you hadn't become a teacher, would you? So I guess you were right
all the time. Just wait until I tell Mrs. Arnwood about
this. That woman has always been full of airs and
graces, but her Violet didn't do so well for herself
when all's said and done."

With a sinking heart Helena realized that the mystery of the past seventeen years had finally been explained. Aunt Eliza had wanted a pretty, old-
fashioned little girl to dress up and be proud of. She'd
thought she'd got her wish, but Helena had spoiled
everything by turning into a bluestocking. And the

harder she'd worked to win Eliza's approval, the more she'd disappointed her. Now she was going to disappoint her again.

"I'm sorry, Auntie," she said. "But Bruce and I haven't discussed marriage."

Eliza's face fell a little, but then she brightened up. "Never mind. A clever woman like you will know how to make him ask."

"Even if I did know, I wouldn't 'make' him," Helena said firmly. The knowledge that she was branding herself a failure in Eliza's eyes galled her into adding, "Why should I be in a rush to get married, anyway? I didn't work hard just to get a 'better' husband than Mrs. Arnwood's Violet. I did it because I wanted to succeed on my own terms and I did. I've got a career that I love and that's enough for me."

Eliza snorted. "Load of silly talk. You'll pluck him while he's ripe if you know what's good for you."

Helena would have died rather than admit that she longed to marry Bruce but feared he might never want her enough to make a commitment. "I do know what's good for me," she said crossly. "I'm fine as I am, and I have no desire to change."

Eliza said nothing, but she looked everything. It was clear she considered book-learning more pitiable than ever if it couldn't bring a man to heel.

Over the meal James could talk about nothing else but their trip and how much he'd enjoyed himself. Bruce backed him up and the two men sustained most of the talk, to Helena's relief. A dark cloud had fallen on the day, both for herself and Eliza, and although they both made an effort, their occasional comments lacked the joyful spontaneity they'd had. At last even the men seemed to feel that something was wrong, and it was a relief to everyone when the visit was over.

On the journey home Helena tried to brighten up, but it was hard. A vision of loving family approval had been briefly shown her, only to be snatched away, and the letdown was hard.

At last Bruce said, "What's the matter, darling?"

"There's nothing the matter," she said hastily.

"Then why are you being so determinedly bright?"

"I'm not."

"Credit me with a little intelligence. You were really happy when you went into the kitchen with your aunt, and quiet and melancholy when you came out. And since we got into the car you've been forcing yourself to be cheerful. What did she say to upset you?"

Helena took a deep breath. It was important to get this right. "It's too silly to bother with. In fact it's rather amusing."

"So tell me and we'll laugh together."

"She's got this old-fashioned idea that just because we've appeared in public together it's only one step to wedding bells. Can you imagine that? I tried to explain that the world has moved on and women aren't in a rush to get married these days. Certainly *I* don't need to be. My life's very pleasant without rushing to become a sock washer."

"Is that how you think of marriage?"

"It certainly is when I view Aunt Eliza. Forty years of washing socks, cooking meals and ironing shirts. Forty years in this little place, trundling back and forth to the shops and thinking a week by the sea every August was a big treat."

"I can see that those narrow horizons wouldn't do for you, but the world's changed a good deal."

"Socks haven't," Helena asserted firmly.

Bruce grinned. "Yes, they have. They're made in all sorts of fibers that hadn't been invented in Eliza's day."

"They still have to be washed, though, don't they? Marriage won't change for women until men are manufactured with self-cleaning, pre-shrunk feet."

He laughed aloud. "I'll bet she had a fit if you said that to her. Did you?"

"No, but I said other things that gave her fits."

"Like what?"

"Like that I'm fine as I am, and have no desire to change. She thinks I'm crazy."

"Well she would think that if she's happily married," Bruce pointed out reasonably. "Marriage can be a very joyful and fulfilling experience."

Helena raised her eyes theatrically to heaven. "That I should live to hear you defending marriage!" she exclaimed. "Don't disillusion me, Bruce. Stick by your principles."

"I said it *can* be—for some people," he explained hastily.

"You and she should have a long talk. You're obviously soul mates. She started advising me how to 'make' you propose to me. Can you believe that?"

"I can believe it of Aunt Eliza," he said. He asked, in a voice carefully pitched to give nothing away, "What did you tell her?"

"I said nothing on earth would persuade me to try."

"There's no need to be quite so emphatic about it," he protested faintly.

"Oh, come on, Bruce. We both know how we feel on this one. If I was scheming for a wedding ring I'd give you nightmares."

"The idea seems to give you nightmares, too."

"Of course. Who needs it?"

"You're right, of course," he said after a moment.

"Of course I am. Now let's talk of something else."

They did so. All the way home they worked hard at finding indifferent subjects to discuss, and when they arrived they were worn out with the effort. They said goodbye with only the briefest kiss, both needing to be alone.

The events of the day had given Bruce a nasty turn. It was starting already, the social pressure to marry. Helena would never pressure him, but the world would. On the other hand, he could clearly rely on her to deal with the world, as she'd done today.

It was strange how that didn't make him feel any happier.

Mrs. Carter put her head out of her kitchen as Helena closed the front door behind her. "There's a letter for you on the hall table," she said. "It looks official. Is it all right if Sally comes up tonight?"

"Yes, fine." Helena took up the brown envelope. Once upstairs she tore it open and found her birth certificate inside. Somehow the sight of it depressed her, recalling the evening she'd thought Bruce might be on the verge of a proposal, only to discover that he had something more prosaic in mind. Somehow that seemed to be the pattern of their relationship. The magical "high" of the first few weeks had been clouded. They were no longer at ease with each other, and sometimes she could have sworn he was avoiding her. Soon, perhaps, it would all end, and she knew, with a terrible feeling of helplessness, that she had no idea how to put things right.

She glanced idly at the certificate and was about to put it down when something strange caught her eye. Frowning, she studied where her date of birth was listed: August 24.

But that wasn't right. She'd been born on August 23. Or so she'd thought. She stared hard at the figures, hoping to discover that she'd misread them, but there was no mistake.

She found that her heart was thumping, and told herself not to get upset about nothing. After all, what did a day matter?

But it mattered a lot. It was like the final nail in the hope that her uncle and aunt might have loved her. They'd done their duty, and conscientiously celebrated her birthday every year, but they hadn't cared about her enough to get the date right.

There was a knock on the door and Sally looked around. "Come in," Helena said. "I'm just making some tea."

She forced herself to concentrate on what she was doing. She was an adult, and far too mature to make a fuss about a childish trifle. Soon she would have forgotten all about it.

First thing next morning Sally collared Alastair at school. "Listen, I've got something important to tell you," she said urgently. "A terrible thing has happened." In answer to Alastair's look of query she went on, "Miss Walker got her birth certificate for her passport application. I saw it lying on the table last night." She took a deep breath. "Her birthday isn't August twenty-three. It's August twenty-four."

Alastair paled. "Are you sure?"

"Certain. I stared and stared at it because I thought it couldn't be true. But it is."

"But that means she isn't Leo at all. She's Virgo. This is appalling. Sagittarius and Virgo are the worst possible combination in the entire zodiac." He struck his forehead dramatically. "I may have ruined Uncle Bruce's life."

"It might not be your fault," Sally said comfortingly. "They could have liked each other anyway."

"I refuse to evade my responsibilities with easy arguments," Alastair said with dignity. "If Miss Walker was Leo, they probably would have got together naturally. But since she's Virgo, their natural tendency is to fly apart. There can be only one explanation for what's happened. Without meaning to, I brainwashed Uncle Bruce into a false position."

"I did my bit, as well, with the perfume," Sally insisted loyally. "I'm just as much to blame. What are we going to do about it?"

"We threw them together. Now it's up to us to undo the damage."

Bruce was back in college listening to a mad professor who was lecturing him about astrology from an enormous distance. His voice resounded around a vast echo chamber, and yet every word was clear.

"I tell you, Sagittarius man must avoid Virgo woman at all costs," the professor screeched. "She is hypercritical and will never understand him. Beware

Miss Virgo...beware Miss Virgo...beware Miss Virgo..."

The professor was working himself up into a frenzy, bouncing about and thumping the lectern. He was no longer far away, but just overhead, and his antics made the lectern topple over. Bruce put up a hand to ward it off, and found himself grasping Alastair.

As full consciousness returned, he realized that he was back in his own bed, and his nephew was standing beside him in the dark, intoning, "Beware Miss Virgo...beware Miss Virgo..." Alastair stopped as he saw his uncle's eyes upon him. "Hello, Uncle."

"What the blazes do you mean by yowling nonsense in my ear when I'm asleep?" Bruce demanded furiously.

"It isn't nonsense, honestly it isn't. There's been a terrible mistake and I'm trying to put it right."

"By creeping into my room at—good grief, three in the morning—and trying to brainwash me?"

"But that was what I did last time—I mean, I didn't intend to brainwash you. I thought you were awake, only you weren't, and it must have gone into your brain while you slept. And it worked, so now I have to do the same thing back the other way."

Bruce closed his eyes. "What *are* you talking about?"

"Miss Walker—being Leo—only she isn't."

"You told me she was," Bruce said, trying to grab hold of something steady in this mishmash. "You told her, too."

"That was because she said she was born on August twenty-third, but Sally saw her birth certificate and it said August twenty-fourth."

"Does it matter? As long as it doesn't say she wâs born twenty years before me, why should I care?"

"It makes her a Virgo, and Virgo and Sagittarius are absolute poison together. It's Sagittarius and Leo that belong together. I was going to tell you about the birth certificate tomorrow, but tonight I thought I'd prepare the ground by—"

Bruce breathed hard. "Do you mean to say that you woke me up because of a load of astrological tarradiddle?"

"But it's not tarradiddle. *I* put you onto the Sagittarius-Leo angle, which means I made the whole thing happen..."

"Not quite," Bruce said, pulling himself together. "There were... one or two other things. Don't worry about it, Alastair."

"I have to," the little boy insisted. "Miss Walker is a Virgo. You don't seem to understand what that means, Uncle Bruce. Virgos are terribly severe, precise people. They can be puritanical and perfectionist. I mean, what would *you* do with a puritanical perfectionist?"

"If that's meant to be an observation on my character, I'll thank you to keep your impudence to yourself," Bruce growled.

"I wasn't being impudent," Alastair said in hurt tones. "I was just trying to repair the damage."

"Yes, well, the damage has gone a bit far to be repaired," Bruce muttered.

"Perhaps if you read the book..." Alastair suggested, producing a weighty tome.

"I might have known you'd have chapter and verse for it."

"We could go through it together and . . ."

"Alastair," Bruce said with a dangerous edge to his voice, "watch my lips. Get out of here now, and take your book and your crazy ideas with you. And don't ever do this again unless you want to find yourself exercising your talent for mayhem in a home for delinquents."

"Yes, Uncle," Alastair said with a meekness that didn't fool Bruce for a moment. "If you're sure you—"

"Be off with you while you're still in one piece."

"Shall I just leave the book?"

"Clear out."

Alastair turned and trailed toward the door, an apparently forlorn, despairing figure that would have brought tears to the eyes of anyone who knew him less well than Bruce. "Wait," he commanded as the little boy reached the door. Alastair turned hopefully. "Yes, Uncle?"

"Leave the book."

It was absurd, he thought, riffling through the pages, but there was no harm in looking. What did it matter if Helena was Virgo? It was just a symbol. It probably had as many good points as Leo. Here it was. *Intelligent.* He already knew that. *Practical . . . can be a worrier, especially about money.* That needn't be a disadvantage. *Can be critical of others.* Hmm! *But even more critical of themselves.* He'd noticed that about her. It made him feel protective. *Their insistence on perfection can drive others mad.* Not so good.

He found the Virgo-Sagittarius section and grew more dispirited by the moment. *Miss Virgo's high ideals make her a reformer, especially of her man. She won't rest until he matches her view of how he ought to be.*

Bruce lay back and considered. Something had gone wrong in a romance that had once seemed ideal. Who could say that this wasn't it? Now he came to think of it, hadn't it always been clear that Helena disapproved of him?

He recalled Alastair offering him a list of other Leos in the days when Helena had seemed to be a Leo. No harm in a quick look to see who she shared with now. He turned the pages.

Good grief! Leo Tolstoy and Peter Sellers.

"I'm afraid I have to cancel our plans for this weekend," he said. "I have to go away."

He braced himself for questions. He had some excuses ready and was only afraid that they might sound too vague. He balked at a direct lie, but telling her the truth was out of the question—at least for the moment.

But the questions didn't come. Indeed, he almost thought he saw a look of relief pass over her face. "Fine," she said.

"I shan't be too long."

Helena laughed. "Bruce, for heaven's sake, be as long as you like. I'm not your keeper."

"You don't mind my canceling like this?"

"Actually it rather suits me. I have a lot of work to do." She snatched a hurried look at her watch. "I have to dash. I've got a class waiting for me."

"I'll call you as soon as I get back," he called after her vanishing form.

He thought he heard the words "Don't worry about it" wafting back to him on the breeze. He stood there, wondering if the scene had actually taken place.

He was a fortunate man, he realized. She was perfect. No nagging. No complaints. No interrogation.

On the other hand, the infuriating woman might have at least *pretended* to mind.

Chapter Twelve

All weekend she waited for him to call her, but the phone didn't ring. Whatever he was doing was so absorbing that it had driven her right out of his head.

On Monday morning her car began making ominous noises when she was halfway to school. She managed to limp to a garage and leave it there. It meant walking the rest of the way, and she arrived too late for assembly. At lunchtime she saw Bruce in the distance. He turned in her direction and for a moment she thought he was trying to hail her, but then a pupil stopped her with a message to say the garage was on the phone, and she had to go.

The garage's message was that the car would take a week to repair. As she put the phone down, Helena noticed that it was raining heavily.

By the end of the day the rain was coming down in torrents. She tried calling a cab, but the rest of the world had had the same idea, and there was nothing available for an hour. She sighed. It would have to be public transport.

She fought her way to the bus stop and stood with her shoulders hunched, trying unsuccessfully to stop water running down the inside of her collar. She shifted her head and nearly lost an eye on the spokes of a large umbrella in front of her. The woman holding it turned and glared, but didn't offer to share.

How had things come to this when she'd been so happy only a few weeks ago? She thought of the romantic myths of her childhood, fed by a hundred storybooks. The gallant cavalier rode up on his steed, defended the lady from dragons, villains, or whatever, and carried her off. Whether he carried her off into the sunset or his castle it made no difference. Sooner or later they ended up with a parson, and everyone knew where they stood.

She was brought out of her reverie by a voice saying, "What the devil are you doing here?"

And there was her cavalier, in his scarlet, shiny steed, looking distinctly unromantic and grumpy. "I'm waiting for Christmas to arrive," she said in the same tone. "What does it look as if I'm doing?"

"Letting your pride overcome your good sense," he answered. "Get in and don't argue." When she was installed in the passenger seat and he was edging out into the traffic, she asked, "What did you mean about pride?"

"If your pride wasn't calling the shots you'd have come and asked me for a ride. Why didn't you?"

She shrugged. "I thought you might be busy."

"When have I ever been too busy for you? I don't know what I've done that you'd rather get pneumonia than ask me a favor."

She didn't answer. There was no way to say that she was sore at him for not loving her as much as she loved him. After a while she rubbed the steamed-up window and said, "This isn't the way to my home."

"It's the way to mine."

"I don't want to go to yours."

"Well you're going whether you want to or not," he said in exasperation, "so pipe down."

Which sounded an odd way to offer his lady protection, but Bruce wasn't a cavalier, just a man in an emotional tangle that was having a disruptive effect on his temper.

It was still raining cats and dogs when they arrived. The old lift clanked them up to the fifth floor but got there without a display of temperament. "Alastair's having tea with a school friend," Bruce told her as he ushered her into the flat.

He helped her off with her coat and felt her collar. "You're soaking!" he exclaimed. "I'll bet your feet are wet, too. You'd better have a hot bath."

Before she could protest, he was running the water and the bathroom was filling with steam. He produced a large terry-cloth dressing gown, handed it to her and pushed her into the bathroom. "Hand your clothes out as you take them off, and I'll dry them," he instructed.

His tone was completely matter-of-fact, as if he'd never held her in his arms, whispering words of passion. It made the present situation easier, but still the ache of sadness in her heart grew as she thought how quickly things had changed.

It was bliss in the hot water, and when she got out, the terry dressing gown enveloped her warmly. She looked tentatively out of the bathroom to see the living room dimly lit, but a bright light in the kitchen. "Go and sit on the sofa," Bruce called. "Tea's just coming up."

She padded across the carpet in her bare feet, dodging piles of books here and there. There were more books on the sofa, but she managed to make a space and curled up luxuriously. She was feeling better, but she wished her damp hair didn't hang about her face.

"I don't know what to do about you," Bruce scolded as he wheeled in a tea trolley piled with plates and cups. "I take my eyes off you for five minutes and you go to pieces."

"I didn't go to pieces," she protested. "My car broke down. It had nothing to do with you."

"Your car never broke down when I was around," he pointed out, with his own brand of logic. "It just proves that you need me."

"I suppose I do," she said guardedly.

"Can't you sound a little more enthusiastic about it than that? How about 'Of course I need you, Bruce. My life is nothing without you'? or 'I don't know how I endured our separation'?"

But she refused to give him the satisfaction. "What separation?" she demanded with spirit. "You've only been away a day."

"Well you don't have to be so dreadfully clear-headed about it, do you?" he grumbled. "It may only have been a day, but it *might* have seemed like a year to you." She continued to regard him with caution, and he sighed. "I guess not. Here, you pour the tea, while I butter you a scone."

The food and hot tea revived her enough for her to say, "I don't know what you're complaining about. You ought to be glad that I don't ask nagging questions about your absence. In fact," she added wryly, "I'm the perfect Miss Leo, tolerant, understanding and undemanding."

"But you're not Miss Leo. You're Miss Virgo—at least, you are according to Alastair."

"You've lost me."

"I'm just reciting what my little know-it-all nephew told me. Apparently Leo ends on August twenty-third, and since you now know you were born a day later that makes you the next sign, which is Virgo."

"And how did Alastair know my new birthdate?" she demanded. "No, on second though, don't tell me. Sally. Those two are the most efficient spy network in history."

"I guess it was Sally. Didn't she tell you you were Virgo?"

"I've never discussed it with her. I haven't told anyone."

Something in the way she said the final words made Bruce look at her quickly. "What is it, darling?" he asked. "Surely it doesn't matter so much?"

"It matters," she said heavily.

"But you don't take astrology seriously. I've heard you say so a dozen times."

"This has nothing to do with astrology, Bruce. I just feel—I don't know how to put it—deserted."

"By whom?"

"By Aunt Eliza and Uncle James, I suppose. I always knew they didn't care for me very much. Now I know they didn't even bother to get my birthday right. Maybe that shouldn't hurt after all this time, but it does." Her voice ended on a little catch, and Bruce immediately put his arms around her, drawing her close to him and stroking her damp hair. "I know I'm making a silly fuss about nothing," she said huskily.

"No, you're not," he said at once. "Little things like that can hurt damnably. Logic doesn't come into it. Go on, darling. Have a good cry if you want to."

"Of course I'm not going to cry," she said, regaining some of her composure.

"Don't sound as though I'd suggested some unspeakable crime. What's wrong with a good cry if you feel like it? It's better than bottling it up and going around tense and miserable the way you've been."

"Oh dear. Was it that obvious?"

"I kept wanting to ask what was making you so unhappy, but you wouldn't let me get near you."

"I thought I could cope alone, but I guess I didn't do it very well. Look." She drew away from him and reached for her purse, producing the birth certificate. "I should have sent this off to the passport office but I can't let it go. It has a horrible fascination for me. I keep it in my purse and every so often I take it out and look at it. I think I'm still trying to accept the truth."

Bruce took the birth certificate from her and glanced at it casually. Then, something he saw written there made him frown. "Your mother's maiden name was Caroline Ross," he mused. "It's strange, but I'm sure I've heard that name somewhere before."

"It must be quite a common name," Helena said quickly.

"Yes, but I've heard it recently... if only I could remember..."

Inwardly Helena groaned. How could she have been so thoughtless as to let Bruce see that certificate? But her Darwin book had been the last thing on her mind. "You can't be thinking of my mother," she said, taking the certificate back and putting it away. "She's been dead for years."

"Wait—I remember now! I reviewed a book about Darwin by a Caroline Ross, a few months ago. What a coinci—" His voice died away as he saw her pale face with its look of desperation. There was total silence before he said, "Am I imagining things, darling?"

"No, you're not imagining things," she said. "It was me." In a bleak voice, she recited, "'It's a pity this book was ever published. The author has tried to make a complicated subject accessible to children. This is a laudable ambition but unfortunately she's gone too far, and simplified everything to the point of uselessness.'"

"Ouch!" Bruce closed his eyes in pain and turned his head away. "Did I really say that?"

"And a lot more, including, 'I should be sorry to see this work in any school library.' You made very sure of that. A wholesaler canceled his order the same day."

"Darling, I wasn't being deliberately nasty—"

"I know you weren't. You were just telling the truth as you saw it. I don't blame you. In fact, I think you were right. I re-read it the other day, and it's not so

good. I just didn't ever want you to find out that I was
the idiot who wrote it.''

"You're not an idiot just because your first book
was a bit raw. You'll find your feet.''

"You don't understand, do you? It's not just a bad
review. It's *your* bad review. It's depressing to know
you have such a poor opinion of my abilities, and even
more depressing to know that you're right.''

"Tosh!'' he said robustly. "I don't have a poor
opinion of your abilities. I think you're a terrific
teacher. It's just that writing a book is a different skill,
one you haven't quite mastered yet. But you will. Your
next book will be miles better. And I'll—'' he stopped.

It had been on the tip of his tongue to say he'd give
it a good review, but the words choked him. When the
time came he would have to tell the truth, whatever the
truth was.

"You'll what?'' she said, challenging him.

"On second thought, I won't review it,'' he said
hastily. "Where you're concerned I lost my scholarly
impartiality long ago. But I could—''

Again he checked himself. He'd been about to say
that he could give her some useful tips about the me-
chanics of writing, but this, too, was a mine field.

"Yes?'' she queried.

"Nothing,'' he said hastily.

In the awkward silence that followed he could feel
himself being drawn inexorably toward the edge of a
cliff. He didn't want to look over it, but his options
were narrowing fast. Helena's face still bore a look of
weary unhappiness that tore at his heart, and it was
borne in on him that he would do anything—*anything at all*—to lift that look and see her smile again.

Even if it meant letting her into the secret that he'd once vowed no living soul would ever share. What, after all, was a vow? Something that crumbled to dust when you met the one person who could understand.

"Right," he said at last. "Drastic measures are called for."

"What does that mean?" she asked apprehensively.

"I'm going to show you something that...well, wait and see."

He took out a bunch of keys and opened his desk, then another little locked drawer inside the desk. From it he removed a cash box and unlocked that, too. Helena watched these preparations, wondering what kind of secret they heralded.

Bruce brought the cash box over to the sofa and sat beside her. The lid stuck as if it hadn't been opened for a long time, but at last it gave way and Helena could see inside. The box was empty except for one scrap of yellowing newspaper, which Bruce took out and handed to her in silence.

Helena took it and began to read. As she read she grew very still, hardly able to believe what her eyes told her. The clipping bore a date twelve years ago, and was a review of a book called *On the Edge of the Truth* by Bruce Venables. The critic had been coldly savage.

Facile...juvenile...pretentious...the outpourings of a vain, immature mind... As Helena read the words she shuddered in sympathy.

"I'd just achieved honors at university," Bruce recalled, "and I was full of myself—something that this fellow spotted at once."

"I think he was thoroughly cruel," she said indignantly.

Bruce smiled and kissed her. "Not cruel—accurate," he said. "I thought the world was waiting with bated breath for me to hand down wisdom from the mountain. It was just as well that he knocked it all out of me. I was a rather intolerable character."

"Not that I saw it that way at the time. When I read those words I wanted to creep away and die of shame. For years afterward the memory of them could make me shudder. It was only a small circulation literary magazine. Very few people saw it. I spent a fortune buying up as many copies as I could and destroying them. I couldn't hide the truth from myself, though. I kept this one. I don't know why, except that I couldn't help it. Sometimes I take it out and read it, although I don't need to by now."

"After a while you know it by heart," Helena said. "Yet it still has a horrible fascination."

They looked at each other, bound by fellow feeling. "It's like you said," Bruce told her, "a painful tooth that you have to keep prodding. But I've never shown it to anybody until now. I had to make you realize that it isn't the end of the world." He slipped an arm around her. "Don't despair about a bad review, darling," he said tenderly. "Just join the club."

She smiled shakily and rested her head on his shoulder. "I felt terribly rejected," she said. "And it mattered. But I guess I was reading too much into it."

"Far too much," he said, caressing her hair.

"I've always wondered what you'd say if you discovered that I was the writer you dismissed like that— what it would make you feel."

"It makes me feel that I can't forgive myself for hurting you," he said. But then his incurable honesty grabbed him by the throat and made him add, "Just the same..."

"Just the same," Helena said, raising her head to look at him. "If you had to do it again, knowing me as you do now, what would you do?"

"Darling, don't ask me that," he pleaded.

"But I am asking," she told him implacably. "And I want an answer."

He sighed. "All right. If you insist, here it is. I'd do exactly the same. I wouldn't change a word."

He held onto her as he spoke, fearing that indignation might make her jump up and leave him. But she only smiled in a way that made his heart turn over, and said, "That's a relief."

"A relief?" he echoed, wondering if he was hearing right. "You mean you don't mind?"

"I'd never have forgiven you if I thought you'd make concessions with the truth, just for me. I couldn't bear making you less true to yoursel—"

His mouth was on hers before she'd finished speaking, and now it was his turn to feel relief. It spread right through him, carrying him to the skies. She didn't want to change him. His essential self, the part that couldn't change for anyone, was perfectly safe in her hands. And for the first time it dawned on him, what he should have understood before, that to love and be loved by a woman who would allow his true self space to breathe, was the very best kind of freedom. And he wanted no other.

The realization put fresh urgency into his kiss, and for a long moment they clung together while the stars swung madly in the heavens.

"Darling," he said at last, drawing away, slightly breathless, "you still haven't asked me why I was away."

"It doesn't matter," she said dizzily. "I'm not your keeper."

"Yes, but... aren't you just a little bit curious?"

"If by curious you mean jealous, no."

"Oh. Pretty sure of me, huh?"

"Shouldn't I be?"

"Yes. I'm just not sure I like your knowing that."

She smiled and his heart did somersaults again. "Come on, ask me where I was," he urged.

"It doesn't matter," she said lightly. "You came back."

"Dammit, woman! You might at least show some ordinary curiosity," he exploded.

"All right. If it'll make you happy. Where were you?"

"I went to see your uncle and aunt."

She had a brief, mad vision of the scene that must have ensued. What did Bruce imagine he was doing? "Why?" she demanded.

"I wanted them to clear up the mystery."

"What mystery?"

"The mystery of why you're so dead set against marriage."

"*I'm* dead set against—"

"You made it dismayingly clear the day we went to visit them. When you told me afterward that Eliza was planning a wedding you were very aloof and dismissive. In fact you were at pains to show me how amusing you found the idea.''

Helena opened her mouth to speak, but decided against it. She was learning things.

She remembered that day, how awkward she'd felt telling Bruce what Eliza had thought, how anxious she'd been to distance herself from such ideas. She'd thought Bruce would be delighted at having his freedom confirmed, but he hadn't liked it. Truly, there were things in heaven and earth she didn't begin to comprehend.

''If you wanted to know more, why didn't you ask me?'' she asked.

''Because you have a way of keeping your secrets to yourself. It doesn't seem that way at first. You talk freely enough. But later I always find that there was another layer underneath the one you were guarding. I don't really know what you think about marriage. All I know is what you said that day, and it wasn't encouraging.''

''So what did Aunt Eliza say?''

''She's as troubled as I am. We had a long talk. She was a little sad because she said that although they'd always loved you, all *you* seemed to want was to get away from them.''

''*What?*''

''All that hard work you did as a child, they interpret that as a rejection. They knew you were never going to make a brilliant career in Havering, and it just seemed to them that you were working to escape.''

''I can't believe this,'' she breathed. ''All I wanted was for them to love me. I was trying to earn their love.''

"But, darling, you don't have to earn love by passing exams, or by writing books. It's either there or it isn't—and theirs has always been there."

Helena dropped her head into her hands. "I'm just a failure all around."

"That depends on you," Bruce said. He moved to draw her against him, but was stopped by the sound of a key turning in the front door. "What the devil?" he demanded as footsteps came down the hall.

"It's me, Uncle." Alastair's voice reached them through the door a moment before he opened it, giving them just enough time to jump apart.

He stopped on the threshold at the sight of Helena. "Good evening, Miss Walker," he said politely, but Helena could sense that he regarded her with disfavor. Being a Virgo instead of a Leo was evidently a crime.

"What are you doing home so soon?" Bruce asked, somewhat raggedly.

"I came to get a book I promised to lend Sally. I meant to take it with me but I forgot."

"Couldn't it have waited until next time?"

"No, Sally's studying Darwin right now, and I've told her how terrific it is and—"

Both heads went up sharply, but it was Bruce who spoke. "Darwin? Did you say Darwin?"

"Yes. It's a biography by Caroline Ross and it's great. Why are you staring at me like that? Oh, yes, I see. It's your review copy and I took it without telling you. I'm sorry about that, but I just started reading it one day and I couldn't put it down."

"You didn't find it oversimple?" Helena asked, avoiding Bruce's eye.

"Oh no. It's just right. It makes everything so clear."

"You'd better hurry along and get it," Bruce said in a voice that shook.

Alastair cast a worried look from one to the other and back again before vanishing into his bedroom.

There was a silence.

"You do realize," Helena said at last, "that if I have Alastair's approval..."

"You don't need mine," Bruce finished for her. He gave a shout of laughter. "I was wrong, wasn't I? Gloriously, fantastically wrong! That's your public, and for him you were spot on. Congratulations, my darling. I was never so glad to be wrong in my life."

"So how about ordering some for the school library?" Helena said practically.

"Ah, well, there might be a problem about that. Some people would say it was favoritism."

"But people don't know about us."

"Then I think it's time they did." He moved closer again and drew her to him. "I read your stars this morning. According to them, Jupiter in your seventh house is going to make today an important one for the rest of your life. You're going to have to make a decision, and it's vital to make the right one."

"You don't believe all that," she protested.

"But I do. Because you've got to agree to marry me."

Her heart leapt, but it was too soon for joy. She fell back on a tone of defensive irony. "Oh really? You've decided that for me, have you?"

"Well, I wouldn't like you to mess up your whole life by making the wrong choice, would I?" Before she could answer, he kissed her. "We're going to marry in Havering," he said. "Aunt Eliza and I have it all worked out. You can't deprive her of her big day, and James's big day, too. He's going to drive you to the church in my car."

"But you don't want to be tied down," she reminded him.

"Don't interrupt, woman, and don't tell me what I want. A man doesn't have to be a fool all his life, does he?"

"No," she agreed, her heart singing.

"You've got to marry me, darling. A pair of struggling writers like us have simply got to team up."

"If you put it like that," she said blissfully.

He began to lower his lips to hers, but at that very moment Alastair reappeared and stood transfixed, his eyes wide with horror.

"Uncle Bruce," he cried, aghast. "Don't—it's dangerous."

"Go to the devil!" Bruce told him amiably. Then, as he lowered his head purposefully again, he added, "No, on second thought, go to the stars—and tell them they don't know everything."

* * * * *

LOVE AND
THE SAGITTARIUS MAN

by Wendy Corsi Staub

'Tis the season for merrymaking, and the fun-loving Sagittarius man is in his element! He thrives on the whirlwind of holiday get-togethers—from corporate parties to the community tree-lighting celebration to hosting festivities of his own. But that doesn't mean he doesn't enjoy those quiet romantic evenings alone with his sweetheart. In the glow of the tree lights, this generous fellow will shower her with elaborately wrapped presents, then wait for his own gift...under the mistletoe!

In Lucy Gordon's HEAVEN AND EARTH, Sagittarian Bruce Venables and Virgo Helena Warner share a love for literature. She'd be sure to delight him with an exquisite leatherbound volume of that Charles Dickens' classic, A CHRISTMAS CAROL.

What gift would you *give to the Sagittarius man?*

The Sagittarius man might be a bit taken aback by his gift from the athletic *Aries* woman—cross-country skis weren't exactly what he had in mind. But when she announces that she's bought herself a matching pair—and happens to have some cozy winter weekends in mind—he'll be sure to warm to the idea!

The *Taurus* woman tends to be most contented curled up on the couch at home, and the Sagittarius man knows it. He'll be surprised and excited about her gift to him: a year-long subscription for two to the local dinner theater. She'll assure him that she's looking forward to their evenings out—especially since the program includes several classic romantic musicals.

The *Gemini* woman is a firm believer in mental stimulation, but she's not opposed to a little fun now and then. She'll present the Sagittarius man with a brand-new home computer—complete with electronic mail capabilities. Now they'll be able to send each other high-tech love letters any time of the day or night!

The domestic *Cancer* woman has a vision of the perfect home, and she's about to give the Sagittarius man what she considers a most necessary piece of furniture—a big, overstuffed easy chair. In her opinion, every man should have one—and he'll heartily agree. After all, there's room enough for two, if they get *really* close . . .

The *Leo* woman loves to shop, and she'll browse all over town to come up with the perfect gifts for her Sagittarius man. He'll be thrilled when he sees the towering stack of boxes with his name on them, and he'll find himself unwrapping everything from mono-grammed golf balls to underwear—skimpy and sexy, of course!

The *Libra* woman has exquisite taste, and she'll always seek the finest quality when she buys a gift. The ultra-luxurious cashmere sweater she picks out for the Sagittarius man will match his eyes exactly...and she'll love snuggling her cheek against his chest when he's wearing it.

The Sagittarius man might be perplexed when he opens the *Scorpio* woman's gift and discovers what appears to be a rock. But the mystical lady will quickly explain that it's a crystal, and it's magical powers guarantee good things are going to happen to him...starting with a passionate kiss from her!

The *Sagittarius* woman knows the Sagittarius man inside out, and she's got the perfect gift to suit *both* their tastes this Christmas. She'll treat him to a series of ballroom dancing lessons—with her as his partner, of course—and they'll find their social life enhanced by the smooth new steps they've learned.

The practical *Capricorn* woman knows the Sagittarius man has better things to do than waste time after the holidays returning things that don't fit or aren't exactly his style. She has the perfect solution: a generous gift certificate to his favorite department store...and of course, she'll be glad to accompany him on an all-day shopping spree!

The footloose *Aquarius* woman goes stir crazy if she stays in one place for too long, but she doesn't always like to take trips alone. She has a certain traveling companion in mind for her next jaunt, and she'll present the unsuspecting Sagittarius man with the ideal gift in preparation: a whole set of monogrammed luggage.

The creative *Pisces* woman has always had an undeniably romantic streak, and she'll spend days working on her gift for her beloved Sagittarius man. He'll be infinitely touched when he discovers a book of personalized coupons—each to be redeemed for a different loving favor, from "three dozen homemade peanut butter cookies" to "one soothing back massage."

Silhouette
ROMANCE™

═══ HEARTLAND ═══
HOLIDAYS

Christmas bells turn into wedding bells for the Gallagher siblings in Stella Bagwell's *Heartland Holidays* trilogy.

THEIR FIRST THANKSGIVING (#903) in November
Olivia Westcott had once rejected Sam Gallagher's proposal—and in his stubborn pride, he'd refused to hear her reasons why. Now Olivia is back...and it is about time Sam Gallagher listened!

THE BEST CHRISTMAS EVER (#909) in December
Soldier Nick Gallagher had come home to be the best man at his brother's wedding—not to be a groom! But when he met single mother Allison Lee, he knew he'd found his bride.

NEW YEAR'S BABY (#915) in January
Kathleen Gallagher had given up on love and marriage until she came to the rescue of neighbor Ross Douglas . . . and the newborn baby he'd found on his doorstep!

Come celebrate the holidays with Silhouette Romance!

HE'S MORE THAN
A MAN, HE'S
ONE OF OUR

EMMETT
Diana Palmer

What a way to start the new year! Not only is Diana Palmer's
EMMETT the first of our new series, FABULOUS FATHERS, but
it's her 10th LONG, TALL TEXANS and her 50th book for
Silhouette!

Emmett Deverell was at the end of his lasso. His three children
had become uncontrollable! The long, tall Texan knew they
needed a mother's influence, and the only female offering was
Melody Cartman. Emmett would rather be tied to a cactus than
deal with that prickly woman. But Melody proved to be softer
than he'd ever imagined....

Don't miss Diana Palmer's EMMETT, available in January.

Fall in love with our FABULOUS FATHERS—and join the
Silhouette Romance family!

Silhouette
R O M A N C E™

FF193

NORA ROBERTS

Love has a language all its own, and for centuries flowers have symbolized love's finest expression. Discover the language of flowers—and love—in this romantic collection of 48 favorite books by bestselling author Nora Roberts.

Two titles are available each month at your favorite retail outlet.

In December, look for:

Partners, **Volume #21**
Sullivan's Woman, **Volume #22**

In January, look for:

Summer Desserts, **Volume #23**
This Magic Moment, **Volume #24**

Collect all 48 titles
and become fluent in

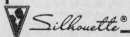

OFFICIAL RULES • MILLION DOLLAR MATCH 3 SWEEPSTAKES
NO PURCHASE OR OBLIGATION NECESSARY TO ENTER

To enter, follow the directions published. **ALTERNATE MEANS OF ENTRY:** Hand print your name and address on a 3″ ×5″ card and mail to either: Silhouette "Match 3," 3010 Walden Ave., P.O. Box 1867, Buffalo, NY 14269-1867, or Silhouette "Match 3," P.O. Box 609, Fort Erie, Ontario L2A 5X3, and we will assign your Sweepstakes numbers. (Limit: one entry per envelope.) For eligibility, entries must be received no later than March 31, 1994. No responsibility is assumed for lost, late or misdirected entries.

Upon receipt of entry, Sweepstakes numbers will be assigned. To determine winners, Sweepstakes numbers will be compared against a list of randomly preselected prizewinning numbers. In the event all prizes are not claimed via the return of prizewinning numbers, random drawings will be held from among all other entries received to award unclaimed prizes.

Prizewinners will be determined no later than May 30, 1994. Selection of winning numbers and random drawings are under the supervision of D.L. Blair, Inc., an independent judging organization, whose decisions are final. One prize to a family or organization. No substitution will be made for any prize, except as offered. Taxes and duties on all prizes are the sole responsibility of winners. Winners will be notified by mail. Chances of winning are determined by the number of entries distributed and received.

Sweepstakes open to persons 18 years of age or older, except employees and immediate family members of Torstar Corporation, D.L. Blair, Inc., their affiliates, subsidiaries and all other agencies, entities and persons connected with the use, marketing or conduct of this Sweepstakes. All applicable laws and regulations apply. Sweepstakes offer void wherever prohibited by law. Any litigation within the province of Quebec respecting the conduct and awarding of a prize in this Sweepstakes must be submitted to the Régies des Loteries et Courses du Quebec. In order to win a prize, residents of Canada will be required to correctly answer a time-limited arithmetical skill-testing question. Values of all prizes are in U.S. currency.

Winners of major prizes will be obligated to sign and return an affidavit of eligibility and release of liability within 30 days of notification. In the event of non-compliance within this time period, prize may be awarded to an alternate winner. Any prize or prize notification returned as undeliverable will result in the awarding of that prize to an alternate winner. By acceptance of their prize, winners consent to use of their names, photographs or other likenesses for purposes of advertising, trade and promotion on behalf of Torstar Corporation without further compensation, unless prohibited by law.

This Sweepstakes is presented by Torstar Corporation, its subsidiaries and affiliates in conjunction with book, merchandise and/or product offerings. Prizes are as follows: Grand Prize—$1,000,000 (payable at $33,333.33 a year for 30 years). First through Sixth Prizes may be presented in different creative executions, each with the following approximate values: First Prize—$35,000; Second Prize—$10,000; 2 Third Prizes—$5,000 each; 5 Fourth Prizes—$1,000 each; 10 Fifth Prizes—$250 each; 1,000 Sixth Prizes—$100 each. Prizewinners will have the opportunity of selecting any prize offered for that level. A travel-prize option, if offered and selected by winner, must be completed within 12 months of selection and is subject to hotel and flight accommodations availability. Torstar Corporation may present this Sweepstakes utilizing names other than Million Dollar Sweepstakes. For a current list of all prize options offered within prize levels and all names the Sweepstakes may utilize, send a self-addressed, stamped envelope (WA residents need not affix return postage) to: Million Dollar Sweepstakes Prize Options/Names, P.O. Box 4710, Blair,[fj NE 68009.

The Extra Bonus Prize will be awarded in a random drawing to be conducted no later than May 30, 1994 from among all entries received. To qualify, entries must be received by March 31, 1994 and comply with published directions. No purchase necessary. For complete rules, send a self-addressed, stamped envelope (WA residents need not affix return postage) to: Extra Bonus Prize Rules, P.O. Box 4600, Blair, NE 68009.

For a list of prizewinners (available after July 31, 1994) send a separate, stamped, self-addressed envelope to: Million Dollar Sweepstakes Winners, P.O. Box 4728, Blair, NE 68009.　　　　　　　　　　　　　　　　　　　　　　　　　　SWP-1292

VOWS
A series celebrating marriage
by Sherryl Woods

To Love, Honor and Cherish—these were the words that three generations of Halloran men promised their women they'd live by. But these vows made in love are each challenged by the tests of time....

In October—Jason Halloran meets his match in *Love* #769;
In November—Kevin Halloran rediscovers love—with his wife—in *Honor* #775;
In December—Brandon Halloran rekindles an old flame in *Cherish* #781.

These three stirring tales are coming down the aisle toward you—only from Silhouette Special Edition!

Silhouette CHRISTMAS
Stories 1992

Experience the beauty of Yuletide romance with Silhouette Christmas Stories 1992—a collection of heartwarming stories by favorite Silhouette authors.

JONI'S MAGIC by Mary Lynn Baxter
HEARTS OF HOPE by Sondra Stanford
THE NIGHT SANTA CLAUS RETURNED by Marie Ferrarrella
BASKET OF LOVE by Jeanne Stephens

Also available this year are three popular early editions of Silhouette Christmas Stories—1986, 1987 and 1988. Look for these and you'll be well on your way to a complete collection of the best in holiday romance.

Plus, as an added bonus, you can receive a FREE keepsake Christmas ornament. Just collect four proofs of purchase from any November or December 1992 Harlequin or Silhouette series novels, or from any Harlequin or Silhouette Christmas collection, and receive a beautiful dated brass Christmas candle ornament.

Mail this certificate along with four (4) proof-of-purchase coupons, plus $1.50 postage and handling (check or money order—do not send cash), payable to Silhouette Books, to: **In the U.S.:** P.O. Box 9057, Buffalo, NY 14269-9057; **In Canada:** P.O. Box 622, Fort Erie, Ontario, L2A 5X3.

ONE PROOF OF PURCHASE

SX92POP

Name: _____

_____

Address: _____

_____

City: _____

State/Province: _____

Zip/Postal Code: _____

093 KAG